Mia Couto was born in Mozambiqu
became independent in 1975, Couto ⠀
become a journalist and newspaper ⠀ ⠀ ⠀ ⠀ ⠀ ⠀ he resumed
his studies, and is now an environmental biologist. He has
published poetry, short stories and a number of novels. His work
has been widely recognised in the Portuguese-speaking world,
and has been translated into a number of European languages. *A
River Called Time* is his fourth novel to be published in English
translation by Serpent's Tail.

Praise for Mia Couto's other novels

Under the Frangipani

'This is an original and fresh tale quite unlike anything else I
have read from Africa. I enjoyed it very much' Doris Lessing

'To read Mia Couto is to encounter a peculiarly African
sensibility, a writer of fluid, fragmentary narratives...a
remarkable novel' *New Statesman*

'Blending history, death, and a uniquely African flavour
of magic realism, *Under the Frangipani* is a powerful and
trenchant evocation of life in a society traumatised by decades
of war and poverty' *New Internationalist*

'Couto's tale unfolds on two levels: first, as a mystery story, for
the fantastic confessions generate a "whodunnit" suspense;
more demandingly as a thematic puzzle' *TLS*

'Anything but an everyday whodunit...it is a novel which forces
the reader to question preconceived notions, to take a second
look at assumptions that normally go unnoticed and to try to
look at the world with fresh, unspoiled eyes' *Worldview*

The Last Flight of the Flamingo

'Couto is considered the most prominent of the younger
generation of writers in Portuguese-speaking Africa. In his
novels, Couto passionately and sensitively describes everyday
life in poverty-stricken Mozambique...ingenious literature –
gripping and mysterious, yet never without humour' *Guardian*

'UN officials, the prostitute, the bureaucrat; carriers of ancient lore and modern ideas chat and clash in this gnomic, comic parable of change in Africa, deftly translated by David Brookshaw' *Independent*

'Couto adroitly captures the chaos and comedy of an abrupt and externally imposed shift in ideologies. No one gets off lightly... The narrative shifts nimbly through a range of registers, from supple wordplay to lyricism' *London Review of Books*

'A wry, poignant fable about any society lost in translation' *New York Times*

'A showcase for Couto's extraordinary vision... an impressive novel' *Miami Herald*

'The book has fierce vitality... The narrator's friendship with the hapless investigator Massimo is touching and complex... real eloquence' *Time Out*

'A wonderful mix of magical realism and wordplay that has a similar tone to Marquez at his best. Couto writes in an idiom all his own that feels authentically African' *Ink*

'A portrait of its milieu: steeped in folkways, awash in petty tyranny and corruption. The book is also a showcase for Couto's extraordinary vision. Even in translation, his prose is suffused with striking images...an impressive novel' *Washington Post*

A Sleepwalking Land

'The story is spare and achingly universal. It draws on a timeless tradition of oral storytelling while firmly rooting itself in the terrible reality of life in a war zone' *New Internationalist*

'A colourful, arresting tale' *Spectator*

'Abstract and figurative, this is very much a fable for adults, and a spirited revolt against the brutal reality of war' *The Works*

'A poignant tale of war and the emptiness it leaves behind' *Big Issue*

A River Called Time

Mia Couto

Translated by David Brookshaw

A complete catalogue record for this book can be
obtained from the British Library on request

The right of Mia Couto to be identified as the author of this work has been asserted
by him in accordance with the Copyright, Designs and Patents Act 1988

Originally published under the title
Um Rio Chamado Tempo, uma Casa Chamada Terra
Copyright © Editorial Caminho, S.A., Lisboa 2002 by arrangement with
Dr Ray-Güde Mertin, Literarische Agentur, Bad Homburg, Germany

Translation copyright ©2008 David Brookshaw

First published in 2008 by Serpent's Tail,
an imprint of Profile Books Ltd
3A Exmouth House
Pine Street
London EC1R 0JH
website: www.serpentstail.com

ISBN: 978 184668 671 9

Typeset at Neuadd Bwll, Llanwrtyd Wells

Printed in Great Britain by
Clays Ltd, St Ives plc
10 9 8 7 6 5 4 3 2 1

The paper this book is printed on is certified by the © 1996 Forest
Stewardship Council A.C. (FSC). It is ancient-forest friendly.
The printer holds FSC chain of custody SGS-COC-2061

FSC
Mixed Sources
Product group from well-managed
forests and other controlled sources
Cert no. SGS-COC-2061
www.fsc.org
© 1996 Forest Stewardship Council

Contents

To Fernando and Maria de Jesus, my parents
To Patricia, my wife
To Madyo Dawany, to Luciana and to Rita, my children

In the beginning,
the house was sacred
that is, it was inhabited
not only by men and the living
but also by the dead and by gods.
— Sophia de Mello Breyner

1   *On the eve of time*

> The earth's been covered with borders, the sky
> filled with flags. But there are only two nations
> – that of the living and that of the dead.
> —*Juca Sabão*

Death is like a navel: all that it contains is a scar, the
memory of a previous existence. As I took ship for the
Island of Luar-do-Chão, I was subject only to death's
orders. It was because of a death that I had left the city
and was on this journey: I was going to the funeral of my
grandfather, Dito Mariano.

I was crossing the river, and darkness had all but fallen.
I watched the sun setting as if it were the last day fading
away. My grandfather's ancient voice seemed to be telling
me: after this sunset, there won't be another day. And
Mariano pointed wearily towards the horizon: there where
the star is sinking, that's the *mpela djambo*, the sky's navel.
A scar so far removed from such an inner wound: the
ceaseless absence of the deceased. Grandpa Mariano was
confirmation to me: a dead loved one never stops dying.

My Uncle Abstinêncio was leaning on the ship's rail in his best suit, darkness clad in gloom. His grey tie was like a rope dangling in the well of his sunken chest. The swallows that skimmed the ship's deck seemed to be delivering secret messages to him.

Abstinêncio is the eldest of my uncles. Hence his task: he was the one who had to announce the death of his father, Dito Mariano. That's what he did when he burst into my student's room at the university residence. His appearance startled me: nothing had made Uncle Abstinêncio leave his house for years. What was he doing there, after so many years as a recluse? His words were thinner than he himself, the minimum necessary to impart the news: Grandpa was dying.

I was to come, that had been old Mariano's insistent request. Abstinêncio gave me instructions: I was to pack quickly and we would catch the next boat back to our Island.

—*And what about my father?* I asked as I chose what clothes to take.

—*He's on the Island, waiting for us.*

After that, Uncle didn't say another word, buckled up in his own thoughts. Nor did he offer to help me pack my few possessions.

We walked through the city, he a little way in front, with stiff gait, but stumbling into gestures of empty formality and etiquette. He had always been like that: at the slightest excuse, Abstinêncio would double up, bowing this way and that. It's not out of respect, oh no, he would explain. It's just that everywhere, even in the invisible, there's a door. Whether far or near, we aren't the owners, but merely invited guests. Life requires a constant by-your-leave, for the sake of respect alone.

The other members of the family were very different. My father, for example, wore his heart on his shirtsleeve. He had been a guerrilla, a revolutionary, opposed to colonial injustice. Even shut away on the Island, in the meandering waters of the River Madzimi, my old man, Fulano Malta, revealed his feelings in every gesture he made. As for my Uncle Ultímio, the youngest of the three, he liked showing off, puffed up and noisy, in the streets of the capital. He had never been back to the island of his birth, occupied as he was between the powerful and their corridors. None of the brothers got on, each one stuck in his own individual lifestyle.

Uncle Abstinêncio, the one crossing the river with me, had always cut the same figure: thin and stiff, busy plaiting together memories. One day, he went into exile inside his own home. A display of temperament, that's what people believed, a temperamomentary thing. But it was definitive. As time passed, they were eventually puzzled by his absence. They visited him. They shook him, but to no avail.

—*I don't want to go out ever again.*

—*What are you scared of?*

—*The world no longer has any beauty.*

Like those lovers who, after a quarrel, never want to see each other again. That was what our uncle's despondency was like. He had had an affair with the world. And now he was pained by the deterioration of his former lover's face.

The others laughed. Was their kinsman tuning his lyre too late?

—*You, Abstinêncio, are a very impersonal person. Are you afraid of life or of living?*

—*Leave me alone, brothers: this is my nature.*

—*Or maybe our brother Abstinêncio hasn't been endowed with enough nature.*

And so they left him, alone and by himself. After all, it was his choice. Abstinêncio Mariano had frittered away his whole life in the shadows as a civil servant. The half-light had invaded him like mildew, and he ended up yearning for a time that had never existed, a widower without ever having married. It was said there had been a fiancée. But she had died on the eve of their nuptials. In this state of pre-widowerhood, Abstinêncio began to wear a strip of black cloth sewn on his lapel, to bear witness to his mourning. However, folk told the following story: the little strip of cloth grew bigger during the night. The following morning, the piece of cloth had expanded until it looked more like a towel. And by the next morning, it was a bed sheet that hung from his gloomy jacket. It was as if his sadness were begetting his mourning clothes. Some members of the family took appropriate advantage: they had a textile industry right there, no reason to weep for a sad loss, but to shed tears of joy at future profit. There was no more to be said about it.

It wasn't just me and Uncle Abstinêncio who were crossing the river to Luar-do-Chão: the whole family was heading for the funeral. The Island was where we came from, the place where our clan, the Malilanes, first saw the light of day. Or, as they styled themselves in the Portuguese way: the Marianos.

There is no other country as small as ours. In it, there are only two places: the city and the Island. They are separated by a river. But those waters divide more than their mere width. Between one side and the other resides infinity. There are two nations, as remote from each other as planets. We are one population, that is true, but two peoples, two souls.

—*Uncle?*

—*Yes?*

—*Is Grandpa dying or has he already died?*

—*It's the same thing.*

I felt like crying. But I was not of an age to, and I didn't have a shoulder upon which to pour out my sadness. I went into the ship's cabin and curled up by myself in a corner. I didn't care about all the noise, the colourful cries of the fishwives. My soul floated, more languid than Uncle's tie. If there was a storm now and the river began to go topsy-turvy, and the waves were so big that the boat couldn't tie up, then I would be freed from having to attend the rituals. Maybe my grandfather's death wouldn't be so complete. Who knows, maybe Grandpa would never be buried? His remains would turn to dust, like a cloud, without any shape. The grave that had been dug would remain for ever empty and hollow, waiting in vain for the delayed corpse. But no, death, this journey without traveller, was leading us to our destination. And there I was, following the river, me and my private tears.

The heat made me leave the cabin. I went up on deck,

where people, colours and smells mingled together. I sat
down at the stern, on some steps that weren't in use. The
river was dirty, sieved by its own sediments. It was the
rainy season, when the waters turn red. Like blood, like a
menstrual cycle that slowly stains the estuary.

—*Is it free, this little bit of space?*

A fat old woman asked whether she could sit down. She
took her time getting settled on the floor. She sat there in
silence, stroking her legs. Her clothes were old and grubby
through timeless use. In contrast, she wore a new headscarf
that contained all the colours of the world. Even the years
etched in her face seemed to peel away, so full of hues was
the scarf.

—*Are you looking at my scarf? This scarf was given me in
the city. It's mine now...*

She invested her head with some vanity, shaking her
shoulders flirtatiously. Then, she sat watching Uncle
Abstinêncio.

—*Is that a relative of yours?*

—*It's my uncle.*

Then, the old woman observed me closely. Her
eyes narrowed. Immediately after that, she looked at
Abstinêncio once more. No doubt she was comparing us.
Eventually she extended her arm towards me and her face
broke out in a smile.

—*My name's Miserinha. It's a name that was given me,
but not at birth. Like the scarf I got.*

Once again, her attention was focussed on Uncle. Her
eyes looked as if they were listening. What was it she was
taking from my kinsman? Maybe his skinny posture. It's

a well-known fact: pain requires shame. In our country, suffering is like being naked – we don't show it in public. Abstinêncio conducted himself well in his melancholy. The old woman put her hand on her forehead, shielding her eyes, alert to every detail of Abstinêncio's gestures.

—*That man is burdened by suffering.*

—*How do you know?*

—*Can't you see that only his left foot treads with any assurance? That is the weight of his heart.*

She explained to me that she could read a man's life by the way he trod the ground. Everything was written in his steps, the paths he had travelled.

—*The earth has its pages: the paths. Do you understand me?*

—*More or less.*

—*You read a book, I read the ground. Now tell me, in confidence: is the suit he's wearing black?*

—*Yes. Can't you see?*

—*I can't see colours. I can't see any colour.*

It was an illness that had come with age. Whether she glanced up at the sky or looked at the river. Everything was pallid. The same happened with green, the bush, the grass – all autumned, ungreened. Little by little, she lost the other colours too.

—*Now, I can no longer see whites and blacks, everything is mulatto as far as I'm concerned.*

She had come to terms with it. After all, isn't it the blind man who spends more time looking out of the window? But what she missed most was blue. For it had been her first colour. In the little village where she had grown up, the river had been the sky of her childhood. But at heart, blue is never an exact colour. Merely a memory, within us, of the water we once were.

—*Do you know what I do now? I come down to the river and listen to the waves: and tones of blue are born within me once again. Just like now, as I listen to the blue.*

Miserinha got up. The boat's rocking made her dizzy. And off she stumbled. The fat woman placed her feet wherever she felt a space, and her presence was gradually lost among the crowd.

One could already see the dark contours of the Island. The boat began to reduce speed. With the breeze on my face, I allowed myself to gaze languidly at the waves. That was when I saw the scarf floating on the waters. It was Miserinha's, without a doubt. I was gripped by anxiety: had the old woman slipped and been swallowed up by the water? The alarm had to be raised, the boat stopped so that the lady could be saved.

—*Uncle, the woman has fallen into the river!*

Abstinêncio looked worried. He who never got agitated, started waving his arms in panic. He looked at the waves, his hands gripping the side of the boat. He urged me to raise the alarm. I pushed my way through to the wheelhouse. But someone reassured me immediately:

—*No one's fallen in, it was the wind that blew a scarf away.*

Then, I felt someone tugging at my shoulder. It was Miserinha. Herself, head uncovered, her white hair on display. She came up close to me so that we were face to face, in secrecy:

—*Don't worry, the scarf didn't fall in, I threw it into the water.*

—*You threw the scarf away? But why?*
—*Because of you, my son. To give you luck.*
—*Because of me? But that scarf was so pretty! And now, there it is, wasted in the river...*
—*So what? Is there a better place to throw beauty?*
The river was sadder than she'd ever seen before. She'd cast that happiness into it. So that the waters might remember, and flow with divine blessing.
—*As for you, my son, you're really going to need to be well protected.*
A seagull tangled with the scarf, its feet brushing against the bogus fish. And then others, envious, joined it screeching noisily. When I next looked, Miserinha was walking away, melting into the crowd.
The Island of Luar-do-Chão must be almost visible, such was the commotion. Uncle Abstinêncio walked towards me, straightening himself solemnly against the wind.
—*Were you talking to that old woman?*
—*Yes, Uncle, I was.*
—*Well, don't. Don't let her come near you.*
—*But Uncle...*
—*That's enough. That woman mustn't be allowed near you. Never!*
Dugouts and rafts were drawing close to ferry passengers to the shore. Some men climbed up on to the deck to help people change from one craft to the other. I remained with Uncle Abstinêncio, watching folk climb down. He always saved himself till last. He'll be the last of us to die, Grandpa used to say.
The night was pitch black, and the launch that came to

fetch us seemed to float in the darkness. Before we boarded the other boat, Abstinêncio stopped me, his hand on my chest:

—*Now we are here, promise me you'll take care.*

—*Take care? Why, Uncle?*

—*Don't forget: you were given old Mariano's name. Don't forget.*

Uncle dwindled into his explanation. It was no longer he who was talking. An infinite voice faded in my ears: I wasn't just continuing the life of the deceased. I was his life.

2 *The awoken name of the living*

The world was no longer a place to live.
Now, it's not even a place to die.
— *Grandpa Mariano*

The launch that had come to fetch us from the ship was
different from the others. In it, I caught sight of my father,
Fulano Malta, sitting on a wooden crate. When he saw me,
he didn't move an inch, as if the effort of just being there
were too much. I leaned forward to greet him.

—*Are you sad, Father?*

—*No. I'm alone.*

—*I'm here, Father.*

—*Without you here, I miss myself, my son.*

He got to his feet, maybe as if in need of someone to
lean on. I even thought he was seeking the comfort of an
embrace. But no. He feigned a close interest in a seagull.
I looked at the bird too: as it opened its wings, it seemed
to rectify our fragile condition. But as he dipped the oars
firmly in the water, my old man sighed, as if in consolation.

—*No one lives by coming and going.*

Then, I noticed an Indian sitting next to him. I recognised

him; he was Dr Amílcar Mascarenha, the island's doctor.
He divided his time between Luar-do-Chão and the city.
On this occasion, he had travelled on the same boat, and
without noticing it, we had disembarked together. He
greeted me with a wave of his hat.

—*What's the doctor for?* I asked Abstinêncio, who was
sitting by my side.

—*To confirm things.*

—*Confirm what?*

—*Look, we're nearly there.*

They were waiting for us on the beach. Almost the
whole family was there. The men who were in the
foreground, their feet in the river, waved to us. The women
were behind, their arms linked, as if sustaining only one
body. None of them looked me in the face.

Just as I was about to step forward, my uncle pulled me
back, almost violently. He knelt down in the sand and, with
his left hand, drew a circle on the ground. There by the
river bank, the drawing divided the two worlds – on one
side, the family; on the other, we, the new arrivals. There
they stood, stock still, waiting. Until a wave washed the
drawing in the sand away. With his eyes on the river bank,
Uncle Abstinêncio declared:

—*Man weaves, the river unravels.*

The river, the great commander, had been shown
respect. Custom had been observed. Only then did
Abstinêncio and my father step forward to be embraced.
And turning to me, my uncle gave his authorisation:

—*Now you can receive your greetings!*

Nothing takes longer than African courtesies. Good

wishes are bestowed on those present, those who have departed, those who have arrived. So that no one is absent or forgotten. Words embrace us as forcefully as the arms of the women who await us.

After these formalities, we walked through the fish market. By now, the market women were gathering together their things, dismantling the stalls. The last fish were being sold at knock-down prices. In a few hours, they would have rotted.

—*Help me, my child.*

For a moment, I thought it was a market seller pestering me. But it was Miserinha asking me to lead her through the crowd.

—*Look up at the sky as you walk along, and look out for a bird passing overhead.*

My uncle made a sign to me to keep away from the fat lady. But I couldn't leave her without doing her the favour of walking through the market with her. I looked up at the sky. A snipe flew slowly by on its return to the tall old trees.

—*See there, Miserinha, a snipe!*

—*That's not a snipe. It's a mangondzwane.*

It was a hamerkop, a creature covered in legends and curses. Miserinha recognised it without even raising her eyes from the ground.

—*Listen carefully in case it sings.*

It passed by without singing. An icy chill struck me. I still remembered the ill omen of a mangondzwane that remained silent. Something bad was going to happen in the town.

—*Climb up on the tractor!*

I didn't even have time to say goodbye to her. I perched

up on the tractor's trailer, travelling along narrow, sandy tracks. Until recently, the town only had one street. It went by the ironic name of Middle Street. Now, a network of other roads of loose sand had been opened up. But the town was still too rural, for it lacked the geometry of planned spaces. There were the coconut palms, the crows, the slow burning fires coming into view. The cement houses were in ruins, exhausted by years of neglect. It wasn't just the houses that were falling to pieces: time itself was crumbling away. I could still see letters on a wall through the grime of time: 'Our land will be the graveyard of capitalism.' During the war, I had had visions that I never wanted repeated. As if such memories came from a part of me that had already died.

The Island pained me in its sorry state, the dilapidated houses, the misery spilling out along the streets. Even nature seemed to suffer from the curse. The wide expanse of grass made it seem as if the horizon was full of straw. At first sight, everything was fading. Then, further away, but within the range of one's gaze, life reverberated, with all the sweet smell of a summer fruit: hordes of children crossed the tracks, women danced and sang, men spoke in loud voices, masters of time.

We passed a luxurious car stuck in the sand. Who would bring a city vehicle to an island without a road?

—*Look, it's Uncle Ultímio! And they waved.*

My Uncle Ultímio, everyone knows, is a bigwig in the capital, wheeling and dealing in business and dabbling in politics when it suits him. Politics is the art of telling such bad lies that their untruths can only be revealed by other

politicians. Ultímio always spread deceit and seemed to
have profited from it, accumulating alliances and influence.
And yet there, he appeared fragile, dependent on the help
that the poor might provide. As the tractor went by, there
was a lively discussion about the car with its snout on the
ground, its wheels swaddled in sand. But they didn't stop.
There were some who were keen to display their solidarity.
But Fulano Malta was adamant:

—*Let him dig himself out*, was his verdict delivered in
mocking tone.

Finally, I caught sight of our great house, the largest
in all the Island. We called it Nyumba-Kaya, in order
to satisfy relatives from both the North and the South.
'Nyumba' is the word for 'house' in the northern languages.
In southern tongues, the word for house is 'kaya'.

Even from afar, I could see that they had taken the roof
off the living room. That's how things are when someone
dies. Mourning ordains that the sky must penetrate all the
rooms, to cleanse them of cosmic impurities. The house
is a body – the ceiling is what separates the head from the
lofty sky. I was burdened by a vision that would repeat
itself: the house rising in flight like the bird that Miserinha
had pointed to at the fish market. And me gazing at the
old dwelling, our Nyumba-Kaya, gradually fading into
the heavens until it was no more than a cloud among
other clouds.

We all climbed down from the tractor together. The
great house stood before me, defiant like a woman. Once
again, sovereign and matronly, Nyumba-Kaya rose up to
the challenge of time. Her ancient ghosts were now joined

by that of my recently deceased grandfather. And the truth of Mariano's words was now confirmed: I might have various houses, but my home would always be that one, beyond dispute.

There was Aunt Admirança, my grandmother's sister, at the door. She was much younger than Dulcineusa, a daughter by another marriage. We would say, jokingly, that she was a distant sister. In Luar-do-Chão, there's no word for half-sister. Everyone's a sibling, it's as simple as that.

Admirança was the first person to kiss me. She hugged me lingeringly. With her body, Admirança spoke of a sadness that words failed to recognise.

—*Why have you taken so long?*

—*It wasn't me, Aunty. It was time.*

In the yard, and inside the house, everything suggested a burial. Everyone was observing, down to the minutest detail, the customs of the eve of a funeral ceremony. Relatives from all over the country jostled together in the great house. In the rooms, along the corridors, and at the rear of the building, there were innumerable faces of people who, for the most part, I didn't know. They looked at me in silent curiosity. I hadn't visited the Island for years. I could see that they were wondering who I was. They didn't know me. More than that: they were ignorant of my existence. For in such circumstances, I was only relatively a relative. Only mourning brings people together into the same family.

Whoever I was, they expected sadness from me. But not this state of absence. They were not reassured by my appearing so alone, so withdrawn. In Africa, the dead never die. Except for those who die badly. And those, we call 'abortions'. Yes, the same term we use to describe the unborn. After all, death is only another birth.

—*Come in out of the lightning, son.*

Aunt Admirança invited me inside. We pushed through the rain, pressed against one another like two pahamas, those trees that stifle each other with the embrace of their roots and trunks. Jammed up against her, I felt the firm provocation of her breasts. Birds' nests, as my grandfather, Mariano, might have called them.

—*Be careful of the lightning,* she insisted.

I looked up at the night but saw no flashes. The sky was clear and dark. Admirança sensed my disbelief.

—*Don't you know? Here, there are lightning flashes that give off no light. It's these ones that kill you outright.*

Aunty walked on ahead. I was able to appreciate how much her body had given in to rotundity, while remaining firm. What was happening with her was like what happened to the ground: underneath, the lava burns, fire igniting fire.

We stopped by the door to Grandma Dulcineusa's room. Before going in, my aunt pretended to tidy my shirt. And she warned me: Grandma wasn't very well, submerged under the weight of sadness. She had begun to rave even before Grandpa had died. But now, her state was getting worse. She got names wrong, and mixed up places.

We went in to pay our respects. There was Grandma sitting in her high old chair, like a statued goddess. There's nothing so vast as a black woman against a black background. Mourning doubled her darkness and added to her size. Around her, as if in some nativity scene, stood her sons: my father, Abstinêncio and Ultímio, who had just come in. Dulcineusa's solemn voice made the room still narrower:

—*Has anyone sprinkled water around the house?*

Every day, Grandma would water the house as if it were a plant. Everything needs water, she would say. A house, a road, a tree. Even the river needs to be watered.

—*I'm the one who has to remember to do everything. I'm so alone. All I have is this little boy!*

She pointed at me. Her finger remained outstretched as if in admonishment, while the flesh that hung from her forearm trembled. It was only then that I noticed Grandma's hands. I had all but forgotten her ulcerated fingers, made raw by the toil of peeling cashew fruit. Dulcineusa pointed her nailless finger in my direction and it was as if she were pinning some vague accusation on me.

—*Only this little boy*, she repeated in a weakened voice.

Aunt Admirança got ready to go. She was leaving Grandma in the close company of her own sons.

—*Stay here, Sister Admirança!* Dulcineusa commanded. And turning to me: —*Tell me, grandson of mine, were you initiated back there in the city?*

Uncle Abstinêncio coughed, by way of a subtle interruption.

—*You must understand that in the city, Mother...*

—*No one asked you to speak, Abstinêncio.*

Her enquiry had a precise purpose to it. They wanted to know whether I was old enough to mourn. Once again, the matriarch fixed me with her inquisitive stare:

—*Let me ask him: Mariano, my little grandson, have you been circumcertified?*

I shook my head in denial. My father saw how embarrassed I was. Silently, he pleaded for patience with a mere roll of his eyes. Grandma continued:

—*And answer me this: have you ever made a girl pregnant?*

Abstinêncio interrupted her yet again:

—*Mother, the boy has his own ways...*

—*Who are your girlfriends?* The old woman insisted.

We all felt awkward. My father suggested jokingly:

—*Now now, Mother. It might be better if he told you what his illnesses were...*

—*Girlfriends are illnesses*, Grandma corrected him.

I didn't get as far as uttering a word. The conversation rolled around among the tiny circle of those who had the authority of speech, with words of obedience and respect. Everything was slow, so as to pay heed to silent omens. After a long pause, Grandma continued:

—*I'm not asking all this for nothing. It's to know whether you can go to the funeral or not.*

—*I understand, Grandma.*

—*Don't say you understand because you don't under-stand anything. You've been away too long.*

—*That's so, Grandma.*

—*Your grandfather wanted you to take charge of the ceremonies.*

My father got to his feet, no longer able to contain himself. Abstinêncio pulled him so as to make him sit down again, in silent submission. Anger and incredulity vied with each other on the faces of my uncles. Had Grandpa really said that I should take such a leading role in family matters? That I should be the master of ceremonies, in full knowledge that it would be a grave offence against tradition? There were the elders, who had the competence accorded by age.

—*Well, what we need to know is whether he's really dead.*

—*He is dead,* Dulcineusa declared. —*It is you, my little Mariano, who must be master of ceremonies.*

—*What ceremonies?* Abstinêncio asked. —*If he's not really dead, what ceremonies are we talking about?*

Grandma waved her arm to put an end to the conversation. She ordered everyone to be quiet, and to sit down again.

—*I don't trust anyone else. You're the only one I have any confidence in, my grandson.*

Then she jangled a bag that she carried on her waist, and asked:

—*Do you know what this bag is?*

—*No, Grandma, I don't.*

—*This is where I keep all the keys to Nyumba-Kaya. You're going to keep these keys, Mariano.*

I tried to avoid the responsibility. How could I accept an honour for which others were more qualified? But Dulcineusa neither ceded nor conceded.

—*Take it. And keep it well hidden. Look after this house, my little grandson.*

She stretched out her arm for me to receive the bunch of keys. And I, tight-lipped, obeyed my grandmother's command. Aren't keeping quiet and remaining speechless one and the same thing? Grandma was burdened by a deep, ancient feeling, a fear rooted in what she had seen and now guessed might be repeated. Namely, that other relatives would come and dispute our assets, lay claim to an inheritance, scavenge for wealth.

—*The others are bound to come, those from Mariano's side of the family. They'll come looking for things, quarrelling over money.*

—*We'll talk to them, Grandma.*

—*You don't know what your race is like, my son. They look at me and see a woman. I'm a widow, you don't know what that is like, child.*

To be old and a widow is to be ripe for blame. They would certainly suspect that Grandma might be the perpetrator of witchcraft. Mariano's moribund state would be the work of Dulcineusa. All of a sudden, Grandma would turn into a stranger, an intruder and a rival.

—*I don't want them here, do you hear, Mariano?*

—*I heard you.*

—*You're the one my Mariano chose. To defend me, to defend the women, and defend Nyumba-Kaya. That's why I'm giving you these keys.*

Sweat ran down the matriarch's chest, its drops hurrying into the chasm between her bulbous breasts. Abstinêncio gestured as if asking to speak. He was afraid his mother was getting too tired in the stuffy atmosphere of the room.

—*Now you are a widow, you…*

—*I've always been a widow.*

—*But, Mother, you can't…*

—*Now leave me, children. Leave me because they're calling me.*

Grandma seemed overcome by a sudden fatigue. Her

head drooped on to her left shoulder and she fell into
a deep sleep. Everyone remained silent, watching over
their old mother. But not a few minutes had passed when
Dulcineusa awoke, confused.

—*I want to go*, she complained.

—*Where to, Mama?*

—*I want to go home.*

—*But you are at home...*

No, she wasn't. Her gaze seemed inexplicably estranged.
She had lost any sense of familiarity with her own home.

—*Take me away, children, I beg you. Take me to my home.*

Her sons glanced at each other awkwardly. Where to?
Dulcineusa's look made them afraid, focussed as it was on
invisible beings.

—*My sister? Where's my sister? Take me to my sister's house.*

—*Mama, your sister Admirança is right here, you don't
have any other sister...*

Admirança took charge of Dulcineusa and told us to
leave. She would put the old matriarch to bed, and maybe
she would wake up in a calmer state. Rest could only do
her good. For she was the one who would have to see to her
dead husband: wash him, shave him, change his clothes.

We left the room. Uncle Abstinêncio leaned against
the door, using his body to shut it. And it was he who
spoke first:

—*As far as I'm concerned, all her ravings are put on.*

—*What do you mean, put on?*

—*Mama is scared of being labelled a witch.*

In the room where we all went to sit down, we saw the
doctor. Everyone looked solemnly at Amílcar Mascarenha.

As always, the Goan was wearing slippers, which made his trousers look even shorter. He had a glass of red wine next to him. We sat down and remained silent. Until my father, wiping his brow with a handkerchief, decided to speak:

—*Well then, doctor?*

—*Well what?*

The doctor shook his head, deadpan. Countless times, he had leaned over Grandpa, taken his pulse, raised his eyelid, felt his chest. And here he was again, subjecting himself to the same questions:

—*Is he dead, doctor?*

—*He's clinically dead.*

—*What do you mean clinically? Is he dead or not?*

—*I've already told you: he's in a cataleptic state.*

—*What state?*

Amílcar raised his eyes to the ceiling, while he nervously ran his fingers round the rim of his glass, which by now was empty.

—*Can't anyone give me a refill?*

—*Explain things better, doctor, we're not used to such complicated terms. Tell us one thing: is he breathing? Is his heart beating?*

—*He's breathing, but almost imperceptibly. And his pulse is so weak that you can hardly feel it.*

The tense air was filled with silence. The doctor drained the last drop from his glass indicating that he needed it replenished. Uncle Ultímio shook his head nervously. It was clear he disliked the Goan. My father, pacing round the room, was walking off his impatience. Abstinêncio was the only one who remained impassive.

—*This fellow doesn't know anything*, Ultímio burst out.

—*Have some respect for the doctor, brother*, Abstinêncio chided him.

—*Well, let him clarify one thing for me: am I clinically alive?*

—*Can I please have some more wine, gentlemen.*

—*Don't give the fellow anything. He doesn't deserve any respect at all. What sort of a doctor are you anyway?*

Uncle Ultímio hammered in his scorn yet again: *clinically dead, clinically dead!* Abstinêncio, a distant look on his face, still managed to smile:

—*Only our father could play such a trick on us...*

—*Ah yes! Mariano!* they lamented in a chorus.

While he was alive, he said he was dead. Now he was dead he obstinately resisted dying completely. This time, Fulano Malta was the one to insist on an explanation:

—*What might happen now, doctor? Could he come round, come back to life again? Or will he start to rot?*

—*I don't know, I've never seen a case like this before...*

—*He doesn't know, see, he doesn't know*, complained Ultímio. —*But I need to plan my life, I've got things to do back in the city, my business dealings, my political obligations.*

—*Honestly, my dear Ultímio, talking of business at a time like this...*

—*We can't stick around here for ever waiting for Father to die once and for all. Listen, as far as I'm concerned, he's dead. He's always been dead.*

—*Maybe the best thing to do would be to take him to the morgue.*

—*What morgue? There isn't even a hospital here.*

—*But Father can't stay here like this, without being buried or resuscitated. We could at least put him in the fridge down at the fish processing plant.*

—*I'm sorry, Ultímio, but I just can't see Father deep frozen among sea bass, garoupa and shrimp. That would be enough to kill him off right away...*

The doctor asked for calm and for time. And another glass as a special favour. He continued to describe Grandpa Mariano's state in ever more professional terms. He was an asymptomatic carrier of life. And as such, the doctor stated, the dying man didn't differ greatly from others, who were assumed alive and well. Like Uncle Abstinêncio, for example. And, pleased with himself, he laughed.

—*Tell us another thing, doctor. Today, you started to smell our father's mouth, like a dog having a good sniff. What was all that sniffing for?*

—*That's just a routine measure. A doctor does that as a matter of course...*

—*Tell us the truth, doctor...*

—*I thought I smelled something strange...*

—*Strange?*

—*A smell of poison.*

My uncles looked at me as one. They seemed concerned to know whether I had heard the doctor's words. From the silence, it appeared they didn't want me there. So I slipped out of the room. I had decided one thing: I was going where I was forbidden, I was going to take a look at Grandpa Mariano.

3   *A sheet for loving*

To awaken is not from the inside
To awaken is to have an escape.
—*João Cabral de Melo Neto*

On the very first night after he died, they placed Dito
Mariano in a coffin. They crated him up right there
on that very table, in the belief that he had crossed the
final frontier. Grandma Dulcineusa wanted to call the
priest. But the family, erring on the side of caution, were
against it. The dead man would never accept oils and
prayers. They should respect his lack of faith. Dulcineusa
didn't respect it. Under cover of night, she infiltrated the
house accompanied by the priest. And they anointed the
deceased, making him slippery for his journey towards
eternity.

On the following morning, however, the body was
found outside the coffin, lying on the ill-famed sheet.
How had he got out? Suspicion shot through the whole
family. That wasn't a death, the usual end of a journey.
The deceased was finding the transition difficult, he was
stuck on the frontier between the two worlds. A suspicion

of witchcraft gripped the family and contaminated the whole house.

This was why I approached that sombre place with trepidation. The room where they had deposited Grandpa was completely open to the skies. Both light and darkness took advantage of the absence of a roof. I was concerned by this lack of protection. What if it were to rain, if a cloud were to empty its contents on Mariano's defenceless body?

And there was Grandpa, his contours lit up by the stars. He who never slept unless it was on the ground, now lay dumped on a table that was skinnier than himself. Mariano had always defended himself in his aversion to sleeping in a bed. A bed was only for courting. As he himself said: you run the risk of falling off or, worse still, never getting out. He preferred to have all the earth as his bed.

—*It's the same with a bath tub, no one's ever seen me get into one of those.*

For Dito Mariano, a bath tub was another sort of bed. If he had to wash, he wanted water full of life, the flow of a river, the falling rain.

All this seemed very remote from me now, a dense mist separated me from those times. Seen from closer up, Grandpa appeared to be merely resting. Was it a case of sleep engendering another sleep, the fatal pretence of death? Or was there, in the darkness of his inner self, a real, but insufficiently strong death? What was certain was that he remained unconscious of himself. And, if I wasn't mistaken, there was a faint smile on his lips. As if the boot were on the other foot and he were deriving some amusement from seeing us already dead.

Looking at him like that, so dressed up in his suit and tie, I remembered his cordial temperament. His daily greetings. That same smile now etched into his final death mask. And we would ask:

—*How are you then, Grandpa?*

Pausing on the tips of his toes, Mariano would give a rambling, leisurely answer:

—*Bearing up, my child. More or less. Look: bearing more up than down.*

The conversation was like a toad's croak. For he, always more thirsty than he was thrifty, would soon say:

—*Take this bit of money down to the shop and get me a pick-me-up.*

He would hold his hand out to me, but it was an empty gesture. There was neither a coin nor a note in his fingers. The bar owner, mulatto Tuzébio, was only too familiar with his credit guarantee. And he had a bottle ready. The pick-me-up – xidiba ndoba – was the most potent of spirits. Tuzébio would then add a few drops of acid squeezed from a car battery.

—*It's to help kick the engine into gear*, Grandpa would laugh.

In those days, there was no war, no death. The land was open to the future, like a sheet of white paper in a child's hand. Grandpa Mariano was precisely that: my father's father. An easy-going man, hearty of laughter, and confident in his speech and feeling. His favourite topic of conversation: women. He made me believe he had kept his potency. He was still a man because, according to him, he had never been given an injection. And he pointed his finger knowingly:

—*Never agree to have one, my child. That needle will enter your body and you'll grow softer than a dead banana tree.*

He confided a promise he had made to himself. Not to die before having his hundredth woman. All his lovers, all of them without exception, he had possessed on the same bed and on the very same sheet. Once or twice he even proffered me the infallible piece of cloth:

—*Smell it! What does it smell of?*

—*I don't know, Grandpa.*

—*It smells of life, my child. It smells of life.*

It was that same sheet upon which his body now rested, there in the solitude of the funeral parlour. I found it hard to see him lying there so definitively, it pained me to think that I would no longer listen to his stories. Having a grandfather like that was more than just kith and kin. It was a link that brought pride in our most ancient roots. Even if I were romanticising my origins, dislocated as I was from my people, I needed that link like someone who lacks a god.

I was so deep in thought that I didn't notice a figure approaching, concealed by the darkness.

—*Who's there?*

Dulcineusa's questioning tone gave me a fright. The idea of ghosts, people who have died badly, still lay within me, city-dweller that I was.

—*It's me, Grandma. It's me, your grandson Mariano.*

—*I don't have a live grandson, they're all dead.*

—*Grandma, it's me, your little Mariano…*

—*I don't know you. And don't call me Grandma!*

—*Only a short while ago, I was talking to you and your sons, Fulano, Abstinêncio and Ultímio.*

—*My sons have died. I'm alone in this world, there's only me.*

—*You're not alone, Grandma, there are so many people here with you.*

—*There's no one alive here in our land. It's one big cemetery. That's all there is now, a cemetery.*

And she turned on herself, repeating the words, her head drooping: —*Everyone is dead, everyone is dead!*

In the end, she sat down, looking vacantly at the walls. Then she asked for water. While I was looking for a glass, she looked at me, scrutinising me carefully.

—*Are you my grandson Mariano?*

—*Yes, I am, Grandma.*

—*And are you alive?*

—*Yes, I am, Grandma. That is, I think so. Or as Grandpa would say, more or less, more bearing up than down.*

—*The others won't like to see you here.*

—*I'll leave right away, Grandma.*

—*Don't go. Sit down here, child. I want to tell you some memories.*

She told me about when I was a young kid, when I still lived on the Island and my mother was alive. Ever since I had been born, Grandpa Mariano had chosen me as his favourite. I had inherited his name. And he, all self-satisfied, would carry me around on his back, which is something that men are forbidden to do.

Then, my mother died and they decided to send me
to the city. She recalled every detail of those farewells:
how the evening air was, the colours of the sky, the early
rising of the moon. And above all, her surprising old
Mariano weeping.

—*Your grandfather had never wept before.*

She had gone over, lovingly, to wipe away her husband's
tears. He had seized her hand violently. —*Don't touch me
now, for these waters have got to touch the ground*, was what
he had said. Seeing Dito Mariano's deep sadness, I had
even tried to console him:

—*I'll be back, Grandpa. This is our house.*

—*When you return, the house will no longer recognise
you*, Grandpa answered.

Old Mariano knew: when you leave such a small place,
even when you return, you never come back. That would
not be the place where my ashes would be laid to rest. It
had been like that for others, and it would be so for me.
And his prediction proved to be coming true. In the city, I
stayed for a while with the Lopes, a Portuguese couple who
had worked on the Island. Then the family got together to
pay for a room in a university residence for me. During
the time that I was at secondary school, I visited the Island
frequently. Later, such visits became more rare until I gave
up going altogether.

Grandma paused in her recollections and caressed
my face. But then she corrected herself as if suddenly
conscious of the repugnance her scarred hands could
cause me.

—*I'm sorry, my little grandson. These are not fingers for...*

Those worn fingers no longer caused me discomfort, so
tender were their movements. I took her hand and placed
it on my face again. I kissed her fingers. She felt as if I were
kissing her soul.

—*Now, my grandson, I want to ask you a very serious
question.*

—*Go ahead, Grandma.*

—*Did Mariano ever tell you how much he loved me?*

—*Well, as far as I recall…*

—*Tell me about it, my grandson, tell me.*

What did I know? My grandfather certainly used to
talk to me. But it was always loaded with lies. Every time
I had visited the Island, Grandpa had boasted of his many
conquests. Nothing I could now tell Dulcineusa about. This
was the commandment he always insisted upon:

—*Always make love, but never sleep with a woman.*

And he would explain: sleeping with someone is the
greatest intimacy. But that's not making love. It's sleeping
that's intimate. A man sleeps in a woman's arms and his
soul goes over to her once and for all. Never again will he
find his inner being. That's why, at night, he would pull his
sleeping mat out of the bedroom and go to sleep on the
living room floor. I could remember his hand beating on
his chest while he proudly repeated:

—*I've never slept with a woman, that's true. But I've slept
in a woman. And that's something that few men have done.*

Did Dito Mariano love Dulcineusa? I could only believe
so, but that was like a participle without a past. I could
remember their conversations when they were already
elderly. Grandma Dulcineusa sitting on the edge of the bed:

—*Don't you dream of me any more, husband?*
—*Yes, I do.*
—*That's a lie. You don't.*
—*So how do you know, Dulcineusa?*
—*Because I haven't been pretty lately.*

He would get up straightaway and hug her as if seeing her for the first time. And both would look at each other in wonder. The wrinkle in Dulcineusa's face would be smoothed out. That same wrinkle that now seemed to underline her anxiety.

—*Tell me, my little grandson: did he say he loved me?*
—*Well, put it this way, he said so in an indirect way.*
—*I need you to tell me all about it, my sweet grandson. Let me explain why: this business of becoming a widow is almost like getting married.*
—*Getting married?*
—*That's what I feel, without Mariano. The joy of only now marrying him.*
—*That's not a sin, Grandma. One could even say it's beautiful...*
—*For the first time, I feel like raising my hem line, showing my cleavage and powdering my face.*

The way they had met was a well-known story in the family. Mariano repeated the episode countless times. But with so many variations that one could never believe him.

—*If I was like that, old friend, when I met you I would have loved you better. Not as much, but better, much better.*

Dulcineusa feigned disdain:

—*There were so many girls in the neighbourhood, and you had to go and notice me.*

Mariano can't have been very young when he met her. Grandma worked at the cashew factory, peeling its acidic fruit. At that time, her hands hadn't been eaten away by the fruit's corrosive juices. Dito Mariano had a cat that was trained for improper purposes. The creature was let loose at night along alleyways and would infiltrate into back yards until it found a young girl who was willing and available. On successive nights, the cat persisted in entering Dulcineusa's house. There could be no doubt: she was the chosen one. Mariano began to appear in Dulcineusa's yard under the pretext of buying cashew nuts. She was still quite slim, wore cloth that suited her figure and a kerchief round her head, with bead earrings.

Dulcineusa smiled mischievously when she saw him step forward. But he didn't display any weakness in his demeanour. He held his shoulders high, and his neck straight. His elegant turn of phrase sparkled like his shoes. Even so, Grandma resisted him:

—*I'm not available for love, Mariano.*

—*And if I ask you for a kiss?*

—*You'll have to wait a lifetime for a kiss from me.*

—*Then I'll wait.*

The advantage of being poor is that you know how to wait. To wait without pain. For it's waiting without hope. Mariano suffered unhurriedly. This much he had taught me: the secret is to delay suffering, cook it over a very slow fire until it disperses and dissolves into the infinity of time. Everyone confirmed: Mariano was a good warbler but generous and honest in his principles.

—*I'm so good I've even lost my character*, he admitted.
—*Goodness has unseasoned me.*

Dulcineusa, however, could never accept this generosity he showed everyone except her. Why had he never given her flowers, brought her cloth, or addressed her with loving words?

—*One can't give names to the stars*, Mariano would retort.

Grandpa defended himself by citing tradition. A man who wants to behave like a man can't give or receive displays of affection in public. Love is a private matter. Dulcineusa gave up resignedly. Worse for her was Mariano's refusal to give up that cat. The woman would certainly like to have got rid of the wretched creature. To this day, Grandma still wondered why he had still needed the services of a girl detector.

She rounded off her anguish with a sigh. Memories did her good. Grandma caressed one hand with the other as if she were seeking to rectify the destiny engraved in her twisted fingers.

—*Now, my grandson, pass me that album.*

She pointed to an old photo album that lay in the dust of the cupboard. It was there that she went, unseen, to get even with time. In this book, Grandma visited memories, relived sweet recollections.

But when the album lay open on her lap, I was astonished to see that there were no photos whatsoever. The pages of faded card were empty. One could still see the marks where photos had once been stuck.

—*Come. Sit here and let me show you.*

An accomplice in her lie, I pretended to play along.

—*Can you see your father here, so light, you'd think he was a mulatto.*

And slowly she turned the pages with those ungainly fingers of hers, her voice a mere thread, as if she didn't want to awaken the photographs.

—*Here, see. Take a good look. Here's your mother. And look at this one with you when you were tiny! See how pretty she is with you in her arms?*

I was touched by the firm conviction she put in her visions, to the point where I felt my fingers drawn to touch the old album. But Dulcineusa corrected me.

—*Don't touch the photos with your hand because you'll spoil them. They're the opposite of us, they fade away under a caressing hand.*

Dulcineusa complained that she didn't appear in any photo. Without any remorse, I decided to push the illusion still further. When it comes down to it, a photograph is always a lie. Everything is happening in life as if for a second time.

—*You're mistaken. Look at this photo. Here you are, Grandma.*

—*Where? Here among all these people?*

—*Yes, Grandma. You're the one dressed all in white.*

—*Was it a party? It looks as if it was a party.*

—*It was your birthday party, Grandma!*

I began to gain courage, almost believing in this fiction.

—*I don't remember their giving me a party...*

—*And look here, right here. Here's Grandpa giving you a present.*

—*Show me! So what's the present?*
—*It's a ring, Grandma. See how the ring shines!*
Dulcineusa looked intently at the non-existent photo from various angles. Then, she contemplated her hands for some time as if comparing them to the image, or as if they caused her to remember another time.
—*Very well, you can go now. Leave me alone here.*
I began to leave, slowly and respectfully. When I got to the doorway, my grandma called me. I detected a smile on her lips:
—*Thank you, my grandson!*
—*Why thank you?*
—*You lie with such kindness that even God helps you to sin.*

4   *The first letters*

> It's not the house where we
> dwell that's important.
> But where the house dwells in us.
> — *Grandpa Mariano*

I was lodged in the same room as Abstinêncio and
Admirança. Uncle Abstinêncio wanted to return that
same night to his hut. It was years since he had last set
foot outside it. But they persuaded him to spend the
night there. Let him stay even if only for some sleep. For
reasons of hygiene, they put Abstinêncio and Admirança
together. The two were close relatives and could share a
sheet. Apart from that, they were siblings and incapable
of temptation. That's how the saying goes: an ox without a
tail can walk through blazing grass. So there was no risk
of any hormones rising in either my uncle or aunt. If a
love affair developed in the house at a time of mourning, it
would spell disaster. Total abstinence is required during the
rituals. Otherwise, there would be a stain on the place for
ever more.

    I woke before morning was up. There was a dust in the

air – could it be light? It was infiltrating the room from beyond the curtains. That strange sensation that I always get in Luar-de-Chão was born again within me: the air is a skin, through whose pores light filters, drop by drop, like some solar sweat.

I got up and took a few steps in no particular direction. My father used to say that upon awaking, one should walk around for a bit to disentangle oneself from sleep. While I spread out the clothes which had lain crumpled in my rucksack, I noticed a sheet of paper with some writing on it on top of the desk. I read it, intrigued:

It's good that you have come, Mariano. You are going to face challenges that are stronger than you. You'll learn the meaning of what people say around here: each man is all the others. And the others aren't just those who are alive. They're also the ones who've crossed over, our dead. The living are voices, the dead are echoes. You are entering your home, but let your home enter you.

Whenever it's appropriate, I'll write you a few lines. Pretend they're letters I never wrote you before. Read them but don't show them to anyone or mention them to anybody.

Who had written this? When I tried to reread it, I was overcome with dizziness: it was my handwriting, right down to every crossed 't'. Who had it been, then? Someone with the same handwriting as mine. Could it have been any of my relatives? For isn't writing hereditary like blood?

I walked along the corridor, which was now empty. I tried to cast off the feelings that the letter had stirred within me. I looked at the photograph on the wall: can an entire family fit into one picture? No, not our African families, which stretch out along endless tunnels like ants in a nest. In the picture, there were more absences than there were those who featured in the photo. There was Grandpa Mariano, proud and upright. What impressed me were his eyes, alight, as if struck by a match.

—*That's such an old photo!*

It was Aunt Admirança who had crept up on me unawares. With a decisive movement of her arms, she took the picture down from the wall. And she explained: the mustiness of pictures couldn't be cleaned with a cloth. You had to lay them out in the sun, for the light cleaned them.

—*Help me, nephew!*

We took the picture out on to the veranda. Admirança sighed:

—*I wish I could lie out in the sunshine like this, without any clothes on.*

She lowered the straps of her dress so as to expose her shoulders. She saw that I had my eyes on her, and bent over the old photograph.

—*I find it hard to look at this picture. For this was how your grandfather expired.*

—*How do you mean?*

—*It was when we were taking a photo. It pains me even to remember.*

At last, someone was telling me how Grandpa had died. It had happened like this: the family had got

together to pose for a photo. They'd all lined up in the
back yard, Grandpa the only one to be seated, right there
in the middle of everyone. Old Mariano was happy,
giving orders, distributing each and every one to their
right place, correcting smiles, and arranging everyone
according to height and age. The cameras shot and flashed.
Then, laughing happily, everyone relaxed and dispersed.
Everyone except old Mariano. He went on sitting there,
smiling. They called him. To no avail. There he sat, as if
frozen, the same smile on his face. When they went to look
at him, they noticed that he wasn't breathing. His heart had
stopped, caught for ever on camera.

In confusion, they immediately called the local doctor.
The Goan, Amílcar Mascarenha, bent over Grandpa,
looking for signs of life. He stood up again, with pomp
and circumstance, and merely shook his head by way of
a negative answer to an unasked question. People began
to sob, but in a self-controlled way. One doesn't weep out
loud, for a tear is a snake that, when awake, swallows us
from both top and bottom.

Admirança recalled the episode and shivered. A tree
gives us shade, people give us a fright. Her clumsily
buttoned dress allowed a glimpse of her voluminous
breasts. I trembled. I was reluctant to admit it, but Aunt
Admirança lit my fuse. I remember her well, womanly in
both body and smell.

That is the most cherished memory I have: she, on her
haunches, in the back yard at Nyumba-Kaya, holding a
chicken by its neck with her left hand. There's the glint of
a knife in her right. Her well-turned legs showing between

the folds of her capulana. She seems to be aware that I'm peeping at her. She opens her legs as if seeking a more comfortable position. And as she slits the chicken's throat, more of her capulana slips away, revealing yet more of her flesh. She looks at me as if asking for my collusion.

—*Don't say anything to Grandpa! Don't tell him it was I who killed the chicken!*

Grandpa was the eldest in the family. Tradition demanded that it was he who should kill the animals. We were breaking the rules, my aunt and I. And this gave the moment its special flavour.

The chicken scuttled across the yard without its head, hindering my view of Admirança's thighs. Its blood squirting blindly coloured my memory with crimson. Until the neckless bird, finally defeated, came to rest at our feet. Admirança placed her hands on my legs to gain support in order to get back on to her feet. While she was getting up, she brushed against me, her hips and breasts in close proximity. Between us, only the knife still dripping with blood. Admirança's voice was an undertone:

—*My oh my! Mariano, I almost stuck this knife into you!*

Uncle Abstinêncio passed by and brought me back from my recollections. He paused and, like someone searching for the right words, checked himself before asking:

—*Have you been to see Grandpa's body?*

—*No,* I lied. —*Why, Uncle?*

—*You remember, you promised me when we were on the boat…*

—*Leave the boy alone, Abstinêncio,* Admirança intervened, with maternal care.

I decided to take a walk around the area. Morning had risen, shrouded in mist. The air seemed thick, almost liquid. There was a threat of rain, but the rain drops seemed to have relented. Abstinêncio had even commented:

—*This place doesn't have a climate any more.*

But now, the horizon was clearing, and a sun capable of wiping away the mists was rising. The guests were still arriving. The mulattoes had arrived on a specially chartered boat – this was the branch of the family that had gone to the North. I even commented to Aunt Admirança:

—*I didn't know we had so many mulattoes in the family.*

—*My son, we're all mulattoes in this world.*

The big house was too small for everyone. Some, the most important ones, were lodged in the Administration building. Among brothers, uncles and cousins, there were even some members of the Government. Strangely, my father found somewhere to stay away from the immediate family circle. It wasn't even a house: a modest hut hidden among the acacias.

That's where I was heading, to meet up with my father, Fulano Malta. I crossed the front yard and passed by the hedge of thorn bushes. As a sign of respect, I called him from outside. There was no answer. I went in, my eyes getting used to the darkness. On the bedside table, I noticed a revolver. Fulano Malta never went unprepared. But I'd never known him to carry a firearm. Now, I'd surprised him ready for anything or nothing. But why was he taking such precautions, a lucky charm on his pillow and a pistol by his bed? Who did my father expect an attack from?

It was only then that I realised my father was sleeping on the floor. I almost stumbled over him. He got up, dizzy with sleep, his hand waving around in the dark, feeling for his gun. He begged me, his arms shielding his face:

—*Don't kill me, it wasn't me! I don't know anything, I didn't say anything...*

When he realised it was me, he took a few minutes to catch his breath, his hands on his knees, his shoulders hunched.

—*I don't sleep at Nyumba-Kaya so as not to attract attention.*

—*Whose attention?*

I knew I was wasting my time by asking such a question. My father didn't want to stir the dust where no one had ever set foot.

—*They're going to come here, son. They're going to come.*

—*But who's going to come, Father? Who are these people?*

—*You'll find out. All in good time you'll find out.*

—*Find what out?*

—*It's not for me to say. I only blow at candles that I've lit myself.*

That's how it had always been. Fulano Malta had always explained himself through riddles. To expect him to change was like asking a cashew tree to straighten its branches.

—*All I'll say is this: these people kill. They killed old Sabão.*

—*Was old Sabão killed?*

—*Yes, they did him in. He who was a man with so much heart.*

Juca Sabão was like my first teacher, apart from my

family. It was he who took me down to the river, taught me to swim, to fish, and enchanted me with thousands of stories. Like the one about the great trees along the river bank that, on dark nights, uproot themselves and walk on the waters. They swim around as if they were creatures with gills. In the early hours, they return to the shore and take their place once more in the ground. Juca swore it was true.

Memories came to me as swiftly as clouds. I remembered the time Sabão had decided to set off on an expedition: he wanted to go up the river as far as its source. He wanted to understand the birth pains of water, there where the belly of the merest drop swells and the process of multiplying into a river begins. Juca Sabão furnished himself with supplies and filled his dugout with the strangest and most unnecessary of accessories, from flags to bugles. He was away for a number of weeks. When he returned, I was the first to greet him, right there on the steps of the quay. He looked at me, tired, and said:

— *The river is like time!*

There was no beginning, he concluded. The first day broke when time had long been around. In the same way, to say that a river has a source is a lie. The source already contains its river, its waters in unabashed movement.

— *The river is a snake that has its mouth open to the rain and its tail in the sea.*

With such utterances, Juca Sabão asked me to go over to him. He closed my eyelids with his fingers, as one does with the dead. There are things we can see better with our eyes closed. At that moment, it was as if I could still feel his hands on my face.

My father, Fulano Malta, waited a moment for me to recover from the news. He knew how attached I still felt to old Sabão.

—*So who killed him? Who was it that killed him, Father?*

My old man had his suspicions. But he didn't disclose them. A pistol had been found next to Sabão's body. The police had picked it up and taken it to the police station for safe keeping. But the pistol had mysteriously disappeared the same night. Fulano Malta shook his head, full of conviction:

—*They hid the evidence, son! So as to protect important people.*

He signalled me to follow him outside, where it was cooler. At the entrance to the house, there was a birdcage on a wooden platform hanging from two curved branches. I felt a knot in my chest.

—*Do you remember it?*

—*Yes, Father, I do. You always had a cage hanging on the veranda. But it was always empty.*

—*I never managed to put anything inside it,* Fulano laughed.

My father was waiting for a bird to volunteer to come and live in the cage. He hadn't managed to rid himself of his old obsession. The cage served as a metaphor for his life, an enclosure where no bird had alighted to share his solitude.

Suddenly, my father fell silent. His younger brother,

Ultímio, hove into sight in the distance. He still had time to
hurriedly tell me:

—*You receive that uncle of yours. I'm not in, I don't want
to see the fellow.*

—*But Father, he's your brother.*

—*Let me ask you one thing, Mariano. Is that fellow
Ultímio staying in the family home?*

—*No, he's sleeping at the Administration.*

—*The people he's with there*, Fulano added, pointing to
the Government house, —*they're all thieves, quick-fingered
tricksters.*

—*If you want to hide, go inside, Father. He'll
soon be here.*

Fulano Malta went in, but I could still hear him
grumbling to himself. He wanted to see what Uncle
Ultímio was up to there, far from the city, away from his
wheeling and dealing friends.

—*You get a better idea of a hat when it's not on
someone's head.*

I signalled him to keep quiet, for Ultímio had now
arrived, along with his presidential manner. My uncle
greeted me in a comradely way.

—*Where is my brother, Fulano?*

—*He's out. I don't know where he went.*

—*It's better that I've found you on your own, nephew.
That we're alone together.*

Thereupon Ultímio spread-eagled himself in the big old
chair on the veranda. He sat there for some time taking in
the world in all its expanse.

—*It's pretty, isn't it, Uncle?*

—*Pretty? Everything here has a price.*

I didn't know it, but there were rich folk, full of pocket, who coveted our Island. His office handled greedy requests. As for him, he wasn't sleeping with his eyes closed. He had already given the go-ahead to some investors who were interested in establishing a mining concern in Luar-do-Chão, and wanted to carry out tests on its heavy sand deposits. And he had even mentioned our house, Nyumba-Kaya to them, with a promise that they could exploit our family's land.

—*Our home, Uncle? Sell Nyumba-Kaya?*

—*Yes, things are progressing nicely.*

—*But do you remember what Grandpa said about the house?*

—*I'm telling you all this because you, being family and well educated, could well play a part in the enterprise.*

—*I'll think about it, Uncle, let me think about it…*

Then he invited me to walk back with him. I went with him, not because I wanted to, but I was afraid that my father would give away his presence. Uncle Ultímio seemed suspicious. He was busy being careful where he stepped, avoiding the sand and hopping over puddles. Suddenly, there was an almighty shout from behind the dunes. Loud voices and figures running out of the huts.

—*It's the car!* they were shouting.

We approached, and elbowed our way through the crowd together. Uncle Ultímio swallowed awkwardly, inhaling a desert. Someone had attacked the car, smashed its windows and slashed its tyres.

—*Who did this? Who was the son-of-a-bitch who did this?*

Ultímio was yelling threats. He raised his arms, promising vengeance, repeating accusations:

— *They just do this to cause me problems. To hell with their envy, that's what comes between us and progress.*

I fled the place, hurrying along narrow paths. When I reached the house, there wasn't a soul there. Everyone had gone to the sandy track to witness the disaster and console Ultímio. I glanced to one side because I thought I heard a sound. I entered the room where old Mariano lay, but all I could see was his calm, prostrate body. There was the deceased, amid flowers and candles. I went up to my room. There, on the bedside table was another letter. My hands shook so much that I could hardly read it:

These letters, Mariano, aren't works of the pen. They are spoken thoughts. Sit down, take it easy and listen. You haven't come to this Island to attend a funeral. Far from it, Mariano. You've crossed these waters to be present at a birth. To place our world there where it ought to be. You haven't come to save a dead man. You've come to save life, our life. Everyone here is dying, not from illness, but for being unworthy of life.

That's why you will visit these letters and not find a written sheet, but a blank that you will fill with your own writing. As folk here say: wounds in the mouth are cured with one's own saliva. This is the task we've been set, you and I, from either side of the words. I'll provide the voice, you'll write things down. So as to save Luar-do-Chão, the place where

*we are still being born. And to save our family,
which is the place where we are eternal.*

*Begin with your father, Fulano Malta. You never
taught him how to be a father. Infiltrate his heart,
learn to understand his fits of peevishness, allay his
fears. Gain a new awareness of your old father. Is
your father sometimes angry with you? Well, let me
tell you something: that's not anger; it's fear. Here's
why: you disappeared, left the Island, crossed the
frontier of the world. Places are good and unhappy
is the person who doesn't have his own, natural,
familiar place. But places imprison us too, they are
roots that bind our will to fly.*

*The Island of Luar-do-Chāo is a prison. The
worst type of prison, for it has no walls or bars. Only
fear of what lies beyond ties us to its soil. But you
jumped over this frontier. And it wasn't that you
placed so much distance between yourself and here,
but you exiled yourself from our existence.*

*Before, your father was at ease with himself, and
accepted whatever you pushed in his direction. But
ever since you left, he has become a stranger, remote
and detached. Has your old man been mistreating
you? Well, he's only defending himself. You, Mariano,
are a reminder to him that he stayed behind, on this
side of the river, tame, without the lust to live or the
lustre to dream.*

*That Fulano Malta always was a rebel. In
colonial times, he even refused civilised status.
Abstinêncio and Ultímio signed up for it*

straightaway, filled in all the necessary forms.
Fulano, no. As far as your father was concerned, the
other side of the river, where the city began, was
hell's lair. But everything he said was like a snail's
antennae: it was all talk. For at the dead of night,
he dreamed of visiting the bright lights over there on
the other side. He trampled on his dream, killing the
journey when it was still incubating inside the egg
of his fantasy.

Later on, Fulano, through his own son, had a
glimpse of his own stunted ambition, trampled on
the eggshell. In so doing, you made him more human.
One of the first manifestations of humanity is envy.
That's what he felt towards you. That's what he still
feels even now.

I've left the confession for the end, something I
had always hidden from you. Do you remember the
books you brought and that disappeared without
trace? Well, it was your father who got rid of them.
You brought those books and notebooks, and he
looked at them as if they were guns pointed at our
family. He never quite realised what he was doing,
he never understood why he did what he did. He
wrapped that pile of books up and took them down
to the dock. On his way there, your father could feel
the weight of that load, and it seemed to him as if
he was walking further than the whole Island, and
that he was walking ashore on the other side of the
river. Instead of struggling under their weight, he
felt his step becoming ever lighter. He suspected that

it was because of what he intended to do. He sat down, still clasping his load. He took a rest, so as to match up truth with reality. But he was affected more and more by a sense of lightness. He was even tormented by a sudden vision: he was flying across the sky along with other men in distant clouds, who were also loaded with books. And he thought to himself: those writings were bewitched. Yet another reason for reducing them to nothing. He ran to the dock and before he could take off into the air, gliding directionless like a seagull, he threw the books into the river. But surprise: the books didn't sink. They lingered on the surface of the water as if resisting the depths, their pages open and flapping as if they were arms. And what your father saw, distracted by his fear, were lifeless bodies, the victims of shipwreck rising and falling on the river's heaving chest. And terrified, he fled. Even today, he is convinced those cursed books are still floating on the waters of the River Madzimi.

Now, you've got to teach your father. You've got to show him you are still his son. So that he isn't afraid of being a father. So that he may shed an even greater fear: that of having stopped being your father.

5 *The immortal father's death foretold*

A mother is eternal.
A father is immortal.
—*A saying from Luar-do-Chão*

The anonymous letter cast my thoughts in the direction of something that I had never resolved to my satisfaction: my old man, Fulano Malta, second son of Dito Mariano. What did I know about him? It was more about guesswork than proof. As a child he had been a sacristan. Father Nunes, a Portuguese priest, had won his friendship. But one day, my father drank the wine that was kept behind the altar. When he was lighting the candles on the altar, he ended up setting light to the church. Those flames had remained in his memory as if they were the fiery furnace of hell.

He gradually abandoned his religious duties. Nunes still tried to dissuade him. But never again did he brush the ground with his knee. Still the priest insisted:

—*How much is your devotion worth? If the stones are pointed, don't you want to kneel any more?*

No one ever told me how he and my mother met. It was a forbidden topic in our household. Just as it was forbidden to talk about how my mother had died. There was some vague awareness that she had drowned.

Fulano's adolescent passion for Mariavilhosa proved unable to bring him any auspicious luck. Nor was marriage enough. For their life together took on a bitter tinge and he, no sooner had he heard that there were guerrilla fighters struggling to end the colonial regime, launched himself off into the river to join the independence warriors. The family had no word from him for many years. Then, after the colonial government had been overthrown, Fulano returned. He turned up in a uniform, and everyone looked at him as if he were a hero who merited great glory. There then followed a year of transition, a long exercise during which the Portuguese gradually ceded administrative powers to the new government.

During this time, my mother had become pregnant. A general happiness spread across her face. Until one day, they began to rehearse the celebrations for independence, which would be declared in a month's time. People were in training for the grand procession that would take place in the capital as part of the official festivities. My mother, Dona Mariavilhosa, boasted proudly of her husband's qualities while he fussed over his uniform. She'd even got her husband a brand new pair of socks. Her Fulano would be the most elegant man in the rehearsal for the military parade that had been announced for that very afternoon.

But things didn't turn out that way. While the soldiers marched through the town in a foreplay of victory, my father took his uniform off and stayed at home. Mariavilhosa, sad, gave up trying to persuade him. Juca

Sabão, who rushed to join the crowd, couldn't believe that
the great freedom fighting hero was blending into the
shadows of his house, unaware of the world and of the
moment of glory.

—*What are you doing, Fulano? Aren't you going to join
the parade?*

—*Why?*

—*Why? Aren't you supposed to be at the rehearsal for the
official celebrations?*

—*What are we celebrating?*

—*Independence! Or aren't you happy with our
independence?*

My father didn't answer. What he wanted to say was that
the independence that really mattered was that which lay
within ourselves. What he wanted to celebrate was being
able to live as we wanted and according to our taste. But
instead of this, my old man just shrugged his shoulders:

—*Yes, I'm happy. Very happy.*

—*So?*

—*But I'm going to stay here and keep my wife company.
It's years since I sat and watched the sun go down with her.*

He put his hand gently on his wife's belly. She sat there a
moment without saying anything. Then she smiled, proud
of his choice.

But later that night, my mother insisted that he
should go and attend the preparations for the festivities.
It wouldn't be long before the flag was hoisted to flutter
proudly at full mast, in the Island skies. But Fulano
declined. His wife, Mariavilhosa, insisted: how could he
remain indifferent to the hoisting of the flag, the piece

of cloth everyone had waited for, the unfurling of all our hopes? Fulano couldn't be bothered to explain. He merely limited himself to these few words:

—*If it's to salute the flag, then I prefer the curve of your belly.*

Did his wife understand? She shook her head vacantly, and tried again:

—*The flag will go up a month from now. Who's to say it won't happen just as I'm giving birth to our child?*

Neither of them, however, could guess what was in store for them on that special day. At that moment, my old man sat down solemnly. And he spoke. Those at the head of the parade that afternoon had never sacrificed themselves to the struggle.

Never again did Fulano talk of politics. What was life doing to him, this rebel without a cause? I left the Island, my mother died. And he sank further into his bitterness. I could understand his suffering. Fulano Malta had gone through a lot. As a boy he had felt a stranger in his own land. He had believed that there was one exclusive reason for his pain: colonialism. But then Independence came and his feeling of unbelonging remained. And now he could conclude with certainty: it wasn't that he was excluded from a country. He was a foreigner not within a nation, but in the world.

Seldom did we talk. My father never afforded me anything but stern company: no tenderness, no protective gesture. When I left Luar-do-Chão, he didn't even go and see me off.

—*Saying goodbye is for women,* I even heard him say.

I stayed away in the city for years on end. I never had any news of him.

—*Giving news of yourself is what weak men do*, was what Fulano Malta said.

Years later, he suddenly and inexplicably turned up in the city. What's more, he put himself up in my room. I even thought he might have changed, that he might be more demonstrative, more of a father. But no. Fulano was what he always had been: silent, morose, turned in upon himself. Above all, he avoided any paternal gesture.

My old man was coming to town to ask for support from his brother, the now rich Ultímio. I can't imagine what rights he thought he had: a job, a business, a relative to ease the way for him. I know that on the first afternoon, he visited Uncle Ultímio. What the two of them talked about, no one ever found out. But whatever happened between them tore my old man's heart to shreds. A final door slammed shut within him.

When he returned to the house where I was staying, my father stitched himself up in silence. He shut himself away in the room for days on end. It was almost impossible for us to live separate lives. We avoided each other, existing there in turns.

On one occasion, he announced that he was going to visit the Lopes, my Portuguese godparents. It was too late. My old man didn't know they had already returned to Portugal. They hadn't agreed with the new regime, so people said. No one was aware of any other, more private reasons. While I lived with the Lopes, I saw that Dona Conceição went back to the Island at every opportunity.

There was never a shortage of an excuse: no sooner had she returned than there she was again on the ferry, crossing the river in the direction of Luar-do-Chão. What was it that made her keep going back? Were they pangs of nostalgia? As far as her husband, Frederico Lopes was concerned, this was reason enough for him to be angry and suspicious. An uneasiness hung over the couple that I was only fleetingly aware of. I recall once seeing a photograph of my mother on the couple's bedside table. I was astonished to see Mariavilhosa's framed face there. Dona Conceição put her arm through mine as she pointed to the picture:

—*She was so pretty, wasn't she?*

Her husband, Frederico, had just come into the room and interrupted the conversation. His voice shook as he spoke:

—*She was pretty, but it's not here that her photo should be...*

—*You know perfectly well, Frederico, why this photograph is here. Or don't you know?*

An almost unbearable tension dominated the room. This uncomfortable atmosphere became an explosive charge on the verge of being set off. Until one night, Conceição appeared, a tear running down her darkened cheek. The bruise under her eye left no doubt as to the cause of her muffled sobs. Lopes ordered me to leave them alone and to go and amuse myself for a while in the garden next door.

—*And take this photo of your mother.*

The following day, I packed the picture along with all my other possessions and left the house of the Portuguese couple. Not long afterwards, they abandoned the country

and returned to Lisbon for good. My father wasn't aware
of any of this, far as he was from the city. Fulano Malta
heard the news of the Lopes and from that time on, he
seemed even more remote, more tightly shut away in
his room.

One night, I arrived home to find Uncle Ultímio.
He had come to pay us a visit. He had brought a bottle
of whisky and a tin of cashew nuts. I greeted him with
cautious surprise. He had never before knocked on my
door. He explained his visit: he had come to meet his
brother, Fulano, because he had thought he should have a
chat with him. My father sat slumped on the sofa, a glass
with ice clinking in his hand. It was obvious that they
had already traded embittered words, for there was still a
pervading heavy atmosphere. Silence lingered like a sticky
oil that slowed conversation. Ultímio got up to help himself
to some nuts. He remained standing, chewing noisily. At
that point, my father shot him a question:

—*Don't these cashews remind you of anything?*
—*Nothing.*

Fulano got up, as if propelled by demons. His eyes
flashed noxiously, such was his fury. That those cashews
reminded him of their mother, Dulcineusa. And that it
pained him when he remembered how her hands had lost
their shape, worn away by the huge factory, sacrificed so
that her sons might become men.

—*Can you still chew those things?*

He bumped into him, causing the nuts to fall to the
floor. Then, he trod on them deliberately one by one.

—*Get out of here right now. Get out, Ultímio!*

This was his son's room. A modest little place that Ultímio had never deigned to visit, not even to find out whether I needed any help.

—*This is a humble little corner, it's not like the house where your children live.*

—*My children are studying overseas, so how can you, Fulano, talk of their house?*

—*Exactly, I can't talk about their house or their lives either. For your children are little rich kids. They have no place in this house, which is the whole country.*

—*I don't want to hear any more of this shit. I came here to offer you some help, seeing as we're family…*

—*We're not family, that's the whole point, Ultímio.*

Uncle Ultímio left, slamming the door behind him. He tried to make amends but Fulano's voice imposed itself, loud and clear.

—*And don't come back here again!*

We had dinner in silence. My old man satisfied himself with some scraps. I listened to him chewing, followed by a full, fat yawn. I started to get my things together, announcing my intention to go out. As I was leaving, my father spoke to me. It was a hesitant, embarrassed tone of voice.

—*Son, you who've got experience of life, you've got to help me.*

—*What's wrong, Father?*

—*Take me there.*

—*Where?*

—*Take me to the whores.*

—*What did you say?*

—*It's just that I've never been with the girls, I don't even know what it's like. Back in Luar-do-Chão, there aren't any.*

I couldn't believe what I was hearing. Then I was unable to hold back my laughter. What on earth was happening inside that old head? Could it be that his widowish instincts were sinking to his organs? I looked at my father standing there in the middle of the living room, dressed in his pyjama bottoms and vest, and it was as if he were the orphan of the house. And for the first time, the extent of that man's loneliness weighed upon me. I felt remorse for not having noticed before the shadow that was destroying my old man.

—*To the whores, Father?*

—*Yes. Take me to the place where they show themselves all stripped off. And then tell me what I should do.*

—*But there are illnesses, things like that. These are different times, Father.*

—*I don't have any illness.*

—*You haven't, Father, but the girls usually do.*

Fulano Malta wasn't for letting the matter go. But I wasn't going to pursue it either and closed the door. The night swallowed me up, saving me from further talk.

I hoped he would forget things. But the following night, he badgered me again. He was insistent, even throwing in some blackmail. If I didn't want to be his tour guide, he'd go on his own, even if he risked coming to harm. The conversation took on a bitter note, until I shouted at him:

—*You should be ashamed of yourself, Father, that I, your son, am the one who's trying to make you behave sensibly.*

He didn't answer. Then, he got up decisively and opened

a drawer. His two hands rummaged around in the interior of the cupboard, his face now fixed on other thoughts. His movements were brief, swift and unpondered. When he spoke, his tone of voice was grave:

—*Look at these papers.*

He threw everything on to the table. I picked up the documents and began to read through them: they revealed that he was going to die. The doctor's prognosis had been scribbled hurriedly: he had at the most a few days to live.

—*Who wrote this?* My voice was shaking.

—*It was Amílcar Mascarenha, a real doctor's doctor.*

I sank into the chair, the papers falling from my vacant fingers. Those sheets seemed to be growing, for all I could see was the doctor's ill-formed scrawl. The floor of the world scribbled with a death sentence. The Indian's handwriting stifled my voice when I tried to speak. I had to repeat it:

—*Tomorrow, Father, we'll go tomorrow.*

—*Promise?*

I nodded and went out. The following evening, my old man was wearing his suit and tie, and had rubbed himself with lantana petals, those little flowers you see all around houses in the suburbs. I brushed away some of them that had got stuck in his beard.

—*Do I look good?*

—*Very good, Father. If I was a woman...*

I took him along the avenue, passed neon lights, traffic lights, advertising hoardings. I was following behind him, timid, almost afraid. Finally, on a dimly lit corner, there she was. Her silky dress heightened her curves, inviting one to go wild. The old boy took some timid steps in the direction of the girl. Then he accosted her.

I stayed there for a while, as if fearing that I would never see him again. Then I went home. The old man reappeared in the early hours, singing happily. And on the following nights too.

And so the weeks passed. As time went by, Father repeated his nocturnal outings, with the happiness of one who knows he has the whole world inside him at once. If there was a lesson to learn, the old man learnt it in the batting of an eye or an unzipping of his flies. He no longer needed any advice. Night after night, there he was, never a moment late, his eye on the front door. And off he would go as soon as the darkness thickened.

Worse than the prostitutes, however, was the fact that housekeeping money began to disappear. I didn't want to believe it, but it could only be my father's work. He had started to steal, and it was no longer just money. Household effects, mementos of sentimental value too. When the meagre inheritance my mother had left began to evaporate, I vented my feelings with all sternness:

—*It's over, Father. You've got to leave this house right away, tomorrow.*

He didn't resist. He packed his things away in his case and asked to stay just one more night. The early morning hours were already approaching when I heard sounds coming from the kitchen. It was my old man bent double over the sink. He seemed scared, he was having difficulty in breathing, and mucus was dribbling down his neck.

—*I'm dying, son.*

I helped him to the sofa in the living room. There he lay, shorn and dishevelled.

—*I'll go tomorrow,* he sighed. His hand on his throat seemed to be helping the passage of air. —*I'll be off tomorrow, just let me breathe easy for a bit.*

We remained without talking for a while. I was gripped by a cold feeling, as if I could foresee a death. Then, his voice still shaky, he spoke:

—*Do you know what the best bit of all this was?*

—*The girls?*

—*The best bit of all was you.*

—*What do you mean, me?*

—*The best part was going around with you, seeking out worlds. We were almost like brothers, see? These last few days, I haven't been a father, in fact I've had no age whatsoever. Do you understand?*

After that, he fell asleep. Morning had already risen and there was I, still sitting by my old father's bedside. I glimpsed the city through the half-open window. Outside, life went on, impassive. That's injustice for you, when the world goes about its business even when the person we most love is about to disappear. Could anyone in Luar-do-Chão have guessed my father's condition?

That was when I noticed Dr Mascarenha pass by among the crowd. There he was, lugging his inevitable black briefcase. I dashed out after him. When I managed to catch up with him, I asked him to explain the diagnosis he had given my father.

—*Diagnosis? What diagnosis?*

—*Didn't you tell my old man he was going to die?*

—*Die? What do you mean? He's fitter than the two of us together.*

I didn't know whether the pounding of my heart was out of joy or not. I hurried home. I could already guess what to expect. Nothing. There was nothing awaiting me. My father had already gone. The door had been left wide open, conclusively. All that remained was a vague whiff of the perfume he used when going on his nightly jaunts.

And the door stayed open. As if, by being so, there would be fewer obstacles to my father's return.

6   God and the gods

That's how God was, for me:
first, he was absent;
then, he disappeared.
—*Fulano Malta*

—*It's not that I'm mistaken, I'm just not quite correct.*

Grandma was insistent. Ever since we had left the house, she had been hammering away at the same note: it was Sunday and she didn't want to be treated like an invalid. In fact, despite her age and bulk, Dulcineusa was walking beside me, firm of step compared to my leisurely stroll.

—*When we get old, that's what we fear the most: falling over!*

And it isn't about falling into the grave, but falling over our very step, as if our bones were responding to the ground's summons.

—*That's why I walk like this, as if my legs were reciting the alphabet.*

She was dressed in black. It wasn't just because she was in mourning. She always wore dark colours when venturing into the street. For years her world had been

equally divided between home and the church. Every time
they told her she would be going out, she would get herself
ready for mass.

Today she woke up insisting that it was Sunday. I
was happy to let her have her way. What did it matter?
Dulcineusa had been educated in a church. What made
her a believer was not what the priest said. But because
he said it singing. Who else spoke while singing? Did any
other white man do it? Father Nunes was the only one. He
sang, and when he sang, in the church, with a choir and a
good echo, it all had the ring of truth. And that gave him
credibility.

— *The cross, for example, do you know what it looks like
to me? A tree, a sacred marula where we plant our dead.*

The word she had used? To plant. That's what people say
in Luar-do-Chão. Not to bury. The deceased are planted.
For the dead are living things. And do you know what the
tomb of the head of the family is called? It's called *yindlhu*,
a house. Exactly the same term that's used to designate the
place where the living reside. Maybe it's not very different
from Grandpa Mariano's whole or partially dead state.

We passed the administrator of the Island. Grandma
stopped, hovered on one leg as if she were about to kneel.
Embarrassed, the administrator said:

— *Dona Dulcineusa, I've already told you not to do that.*

— *Yes, Mister Administrator, sir. Please don't beat me, I'm
too old for the paddle!*

The administrator shook his head. He couldn't believe
all that was a case of dementia. He thought it was just
insolence, designed for specifically political purposes:

Dulcineusa was pretending to confuse him with a colonial administrator. The official crossed the road hurriedly before people were drawn there by curiosity.

Grandma didn't stop talking, convinced as she was that there was no more sensible person than she in our family. What she wanted to say was that I should back her in her main struggle, which was that the dying man should receive the blessing of the Catholic religion. And that the priest should take charge of the remaining precepts and ceremonies. After all, the coffin commissioned for the purpose was still there, at home, waiting for the corpse and for its final blessing.

That was why we were on our way to speak to Father Nunes, who had been carrying out his duties on the Island for over thirty years. I couldn't imagine Luar-do-Chão without his serene presence, as if he had already become the spirit of the place.

When I entered the church, I was better able to appreciate Grandma's determination. In contrast to the degradation of the area, the church was painted, well maintained, and there was even a little garden to give pride to the immediate neighbourhood. It was the oldest of the buildings thereabouts, a place of temperance standing against temporality. In a world beset by doubt, where everything crumbles away, a church presents itself as a place of certain and permanent memory.

Father Nunes greeted me in his informal manner, with his unassuming tone of voice, which made the language he spoke sound more gentle. That peace inside the church always had an immediate effect on me: I always felt delightfully sleepy. I was never able to succumb to that urge to lie down and sleep there for days on end. And it certainly wouldn't be on this occasion that I would fulfil such a desire. The priest took me to the sacristy while Grandma prayed next to the altar.

—*How are your studies going, Mariano?*

He was the first person who wanted to know what I was doing in the city. It was he who had baptised me, he who had first taught me to read. Nunes was like an uncle from beyond family, race and faith.

—*And how is your father?*

He asked me this before I had answered his first question. He knew that my father had long lost faith in the god of the Catholics. As far as he was concerned, it was obvious: Fulano had his own exclusive faith, he had made a church inside himself.

—*Your father fought so that we might all be rich, sharing that great wealth which is quite simply not having poverty.*

They had had serious disagreements. But he had no greater respect for anyone on the whole Island. At the time when my father decided to go and join the guerrillas, Father Nunes was summoned by the family at Dulcineusa's request. The Portuguese asked my father to reconsider. But he did so unwillingly. That's what he was telling me now: at that time, he wished he were in Fulano Malta's shoes. A secret envy gnawed away at him inside. He wanted to be the one to leave, to break with everything, on his way to being someone else. It wasn't that he agreed with Fulano's ideals. His problem was that he was tired. Injustice couldn't be the result of divine command. And yet its institution

had become so well established that it seemed more prone
to bend its knee before the powerful than before God.

—*I can imagine how much your father has suffered by
seeing what is happening.*

But for the priest, poverty in Luar-do-Chão was only
a preview of what would happen with rich nations. The
violence of uprisings in the great capital cities of the world.
As far as he was concerned, it was just an omen. It wasn't
just innocent folk who were dying. It was the collapse of
a whole way of life. It was a pity that there was no faith in
which to take refuge, as Fulano Malta had done twenty
years before.

—*But have you no hope at all, Father?*

—*If I say I have no hope, how can I maintain my
faith in God?*

He lowered his eyes as if he were putting an end to the
conversation. He got to his feet and showed me the way for
us to go and meet Dulcineusa. A strange smell invaded my
breast. Some animal's urine, I was almost afraid to admit.

—*Isn't there an animal smell around here?*

Grandma didn't allow time for an answer. She addressed
Father Nunes:

—*Can I ask for Dito Mariano to receive the last rites?*

—*I've already done that, Dona Dulcineusa. Don't you
remember?*

—*It would be better to pass the oils over him once more.
A second coat. You don't know my husband, Reverend
Father. He's not an easy one to oil.*

The priest smiled at me indulgently. Grandma pointed
to a candle on the parapet:

—*I've just lit this one for my deceased husband.*

—*So has it been confirmed then that he has died?*

It was by way of prevention, came Grandma's reply. So as to awaken his guardian angel. The priest smiled. Was Dulcineusa aware of what her husband always said? For he was forever repeating:

—*Fortunately, my angel has never guarded me.*

Nunes knew that our patriarch's prayers were never directed to any god. Or maybe there were other gods that belonged solely to him. Whatever the case, such divinities must have been pretty ones. For they weren't abandoning him during this time when he was suspended between mortal and immortal life.

We were leaving when suddenly I came face to face with a donkey. I jumped with fright at such an unexpected vision. What was an animal doing in the sacred refuge of souls? This explained the source of the smell which I had noticed a short time before. The priest challenged me:

—*I'll give you a prize if you manage to get it out of here.*

I didn't even try. The donkey contemplated me with its eyes like water in a deep well. There was such tranquillity in that look that I began to wonder whether the church wasn't its natural abode after all.

—*Later, your grandmother will explain the reason for the donkey's presence here.*

At the door of the church, we bade Nunes goodbye. He took his leave of me in the local manner, turning his hand round his thumb.

—*I'm going away on holiday, I leave tomorrow,* he

announced. And reading my face, he added: —*We also have holidays.*

—*I can understand you must be tired.*

What tired him most weren't his religious tasks. It was man's disrespect for life. Just as had happened in the incident of the ship that had sunk with the loss of numerous people.

—*How much we suffered that day, do you remember, Dulcineusa?*

—*Don't even talk about it, Father.*

—*And you say you're worried that I haven't commended old Mariano's soul to God? Don't forget all those people who didn't even get a burial.*

—*That's the nature of money-making, Father: some possess, others are possessed by money.*

Dulcineusa had already told me about the ship that had sunk, a matter of minutes after leaving the dock, overloaded with people, timber and other goods. The priest had written to the newspaper denouncing those responsible. And from that day, he began to receive threats. They accused him of being white, of being racist, of not sticking to his religious obligations. All this had provoked a tiredness within him from which he would never recover. His voice was fragile when he asked me:

—*And you, Mariano, are you going to stay here?*

What can I do about it? I felt like answering. Can one give one's relations time off? I looked around me in silence. Bathed in the peace and quiet of the little church, I felt at that moment like abdicating from being a son, grandson, nephew. To stop being a person. To suspend my emotions

like someone hanging up an old coat. To do what old
Mariano was doing. Or to remain there, frozen in the
peace of that little church, keeping the donkey company.
Dulcineusa told me to hurry.

—*Come on, your grandfather's all by himself.*

I offered her my shoulder to lean on while she
descended the steps. The tractor, loaded with tree trunks,
passed by. The driver waved to us amicably, his smile
growing broader on an already wide face. Grandma had
stopped to shake her sandal. I went back to help her. Her
unfocussed speech took me by surprise:

—*Thank you so much, Reverend Father.*

—*Grandma, it's me, your grandson.*

She struck her sandal to shake the sand out of it.
She was standing on one foot, swaying while supported
by my body.

—*But don't you want to be a priest?*

—*I've never thought about it, Grandma.*

—*What a pity! You're such a good listener.*

The streets were full of children going home from
school. Some of them stared at me hard. They saw in me a
stranger. It was what I felt. As if the Island were escaping
from me like a boat, drifting away in the river's current. If
it weren't for Grandma's presence, at that moment I would
have wandered off along other paths, become so lost that I
wouldn't have recognised the place at all.

Once again, I began to detect signs of decadence, as if
every ruin were a wound inside me. It is not a pleasant
sight to watch time dying like this. If only the past could
be removed far away, like a corpse. And if only it could be

left there, out of sight, ground into dust. But no. Our Island was imitating Grandpa Mariano, passing away right next to us, decomposing before our defenceless, bewildered gaze. Within reach of our tears, or of a fly's buzz.

—*Can I ask you something, my little grandson?*

—*Of course you can, Grandma.*

—*When we get home and say goodnight, can I call you 'Reverend Father'?*

She explained that she had a confession to make on her knees, in exchange for clemency. I would be the first person to listen to her opening her heart. In the end, she didn't even wait until we got home, for right there, she burst out on the spot:

—*It was I who killed your grandfather!*

I smiled, but without really wanting to. Smiling is my answer when I don't know how to react. Dulcineusa gave me no time, and pressed on:

—*I always wanted to kill him, Reverend Father. Always. That man made me suffer so much with all those lovers of his. And now, do you know what has happened?*

—*Tell me, don't be frightened.*

—*Now he's dead, all I want is for him to be alive again.*

7   *An enigmatic donkey*

When the earth becomes an
altar, life becomes a prayer.
— *Father Nunes*

I never imagined how much torment the Island had
suffered as a result of the ship sinking. It was as if the entire
fate of Luar-do-Chão had been stained by this dishonour.
I only appreciated the weight of this memory when
Grandma Dulcineusa told me about the donkey we had
come across inside the very house of God.

The presence of the animal had left me intrigued. So
much so that at night, the creature had briefly peeped in on
my dreams. And it wasn't a nightmare. A donkey's gaze is
always cushioned in soft and gentle velvet. But those eyes
conveyed more than that. They possessed a most human
expression and invited me to embark on journeys and
crossings that I found disturbing, well beyond the last bend
in the river.

I woke up, shaken, in a hurry to explain the strange
sensation I had received on our visit to Father Nunes. I
surprised my grandmother in the kitchen preparing a

meal. I could hear her monotonous murmuring through
the window. Grandma always recited as she prepared food.
It was inevitably a prayer repeated over and over again:
—*Seed in the soil, bread in the oven, a drop in the womb,
this world is swollen with child but will never be a father.*
She interrupted her chanting and I quizzed her even before
bidding her good day:

   —*Grandma, tell me why that donkey was in the church!*
   —*Donkey?*
   —*Yes, how does a donkey get to live in a church?*
   —*What's the problem? Didn't Jesus have a donkey
standing there by his crib?*

   She was avoiding an answer. I was so persistent that she
sat down with a deep sigh. Such a thick shadow passed
over her face that it even seemed to darken her voice. She
told me that I was making a mistake by wanting to know.
As if the mystery of the whole universe were contained in
that sad animal, so heretically placed in a holy sanctuary.
Grandma moistened her index finger in the manner of
people who count money. Whenever she guessed that she
was in for a long conversation, she resorted to this habit as
if she were getting ready to turn the pages of a thick book.

   —*The story of that donkey began on the day of the
disaster.*

   She could remember everything that had happened on
the day of the tragedy involving the ship. That morning,
she had gone to help Father Nunes see to his tasks. The
day had risen, light and clear. Suddenly, however, an
unexpected gale stirred the heavens. The clouds began
to weigh heavily as if they were hangers on which hung

dark clothes next to the houses. Dulcineusa walked more quickly in order to seek shelter in the house of God. She found Father Nunes sitting on an altar step. The Portuguese was absorbed, listening to the rain drumming on the church roof. It was a strange beating sound, like those that begin unannounced, and in an instant, cause the whole sky to dissolve.

Some hurried knocks on the door didn't interrupt the priest's meditation. He continued to look at the candle on the altar. The melting wax paused, like a hesitant tear at the top of the candle. Then it would drop suddenly and meanderingly until it lost its strength and come to a stop in a solid blob. With his finger, the priest would reshape the candle as if it was some toy that he had to finish making.

When the banging on the door became even louder, the priest called Grandma Dulcineusa, and asked her to go and see who it was. Grandma put down the flowers she was carrying in her arms, As she always did, she was replacing the real flowers with plastic ones that people brought her from the city. The wild flowers with which the priest decorated the atrium were thrown out of the window and replaced with imperfectly finished imitations. It's plastic, she said, that's eternal. One couldn't keep perishable things in a place like this. Even we humble creatures became eternal in that sanctuary.

—*Who is it?* The priest asked.

The old woman looked through the spy-hole and announced:

—*It's João Loucomotiva.*

The priest sighed. João was a former brake man who had migrated to the city and gone mad when the trains stopped running. The man returned to the Island, but part of him stayed behind for ever in the railway station, waiting for the slow whistle of the trains. What did the crazy old man want at that hour? When Dulcineusa opened the door, all the priest could glimpse, half dazzled by the light from outside, was a donkey. So drenched was the beast that its ears were sagging under the weight. Only then did João Loucomotiva's shape appear.

—*Come in, for the love of God.*

The old railwayman shook the sleeves of his coat and cupped his hands to collect the water running down his face.

—*Come in, my friend. But leave the donkey outside.*

It was too late. The ass was already enjoying the shelter and resisted all use of force to try and get it back through the door. Its body all taut, it obstinately dug in its hooves. João Loucomotiva gave up trying to push the animal. The priest eventually accepted the natural disorder of things. The ass slithered on the ground and the clatter of its hooves echoed throughout the building. It was its proclamation of having taken possession of its new abode.

—*But what on earth is this donkey doing here? Is the animal yours?*

—*This donkey was on the ship.*

—*But what ship?*

—*I'll tell you everything, Father.*

—*Then in God's name, speak!*

—*I've come here because I was told to summon you.*

—*You were told to summon me?*

—*Because of the disaster.*

The priest pondered in silence: so that's it, here he comes with some daydream about a disaster. It was all part of João's craziness: listening to trains derailing out in the marshlands, falling over bridges and dissolving into the darkness of tunnels. Nunes asked God to strengthen his patience and provide comfort to that derailed creature, as if the church were the railway station sought for so long by the madman. He turned to Loucomotiva and opened his arms, thinking: I'm a scarecrow, so poor and such a failure, that I end up attracting rather than scaring away our feathered friends. And this one who's just come in is a bird, as much of a bird as the real ones, with wings and plumage.

—*It wasn't a train, Father. It was a ship, the ship that sank.*

—*A ship sank? When?*

—*Early this morning. This donkey was travelling on the ship, and it was the only survivor.*

The first thing the priest did was to kneel and cross himself. The silence that fell upon them as he prayed appeared to merit the respect of even the donkey which, with rounded eyes, stood contemplating the Portuguese man without moving. And that's how things were, everything shrouded in divine silence, until the priest got up and opened the doors. It had stopped raining and a strange quietness pervaded the whole hillside. That was when they heard the lamentations, screams and wailing coming from the direction of the river. The women were proclaiming their grief, a sign that death was already reaping its harvest. Dulcineusa dropped her flowers and hurried out. The priest followed Grandma, lifting his gown in order to walk faster. João Loucomotiva then withdrew unhurriedly, at the same time making sure that his four-legged companion wasn't going to leave the church.

Down by the river, a search was still going on, but there was no longer any hope of finding survivors. The tragedy had occurred in the early hours of the morning. The bodies had sunk for ever in the current. The hull of the ship, half submerged, was still floating. On its rusting hulk, one could still read the ship's name, painted in green letters: *Vasco da Gama*. It was the ship that linked the Island with the city, and as always, it had been overloaded with passengers and freight. Everyone acknowledged in hushed tones that the cause of the accident lay in the ambition of its new owners. The names of the guilty parties were generally known but, unlike the green letters on the hull, their identity would remain hidden under a veil of fear.

Now it was possible to understand the sudden change in the elements during the early hours. When the ship was swallowed up by the waters, the skies over the Island were in turbulence. A bang committed everything to darkness and the clouds thickened. A sudden wind picked up and blew through the houses. In the church tower, the bell began to toll without anyone ringing it. The trees began to quiver and all of a sudden, in one single movement, their trunks bent and turned towards the west. The gods were scribbling complaints against the blue background of the heavens. The local population realised that what was happening wasn't just an accident on the river. It was much more than that.

As he took in the extent of the tragedy, the priest gradually lost his powers of reason, becoming as crazy as João Loucomotiva himself. He took off his glasses and threw them in the grass. Dulcineusa followed on his heels to give him back what he had dropped. But the priest declined them emphatically. He preferred not to see anything.

And in this way, guided by his myopia and stumbling along, the priest began to wander purposelessly, as if any direction would do for him. Dulcineusa followed some way behind, saddened that she should be witnessing the disintegration of her religious mentor's spirit. She prayed under her breath that it might be a temporary state but the priest gave no sign of recovering. Finally, when he was near the marshes, he stopped in front of the witchdoctor Muana wa Nweti's house. After some hesitation, he entered the darkness of the hut. He asked the witchdoctor:

—*Cast your shells, Muana wa Nweti.*

Intrigued, the soothsayer looked up. The priest insisted encouragingly: let him cast his shells for he wanted to know his fate, now that the angels had allowed him to fall into the void of uncertainty.

—*Let the shells speak.*

Dulcineusa withdrew out of respect. She never discovered what difficulties the soothsayer had detected in the Portuguese man's future. But this didn't worry her as much as the fact that the cleric had agreed to sit down in the fortune teller's yard. How lost was he that he had subjected himself to that which he had always condemned?

When the priest emerged from his consultation, she once again followed him while gently insisting all the while:

—*Father, your glasses.*

Nunes returned to the church and was preparing to shut himself in there when he turned round towards Dulcineusa and mumbled something she couldn't understand. Grandma took the opportunity to satisfy her burning curiosity:

—*What did that witchdoctor tell you, Father?*

Nunes stared at her with such an inebriated air that for a moment, old Dulcineusa believed Muana wa Nweti must have given him something to drink. After a few seconds, the priest spoke:

—*That donkey, Dona Dulcineusa. Promise me you'll treat it.*

—*Treat it?*

It was never explained to Grandma what treatments were to be applied to the beast. Nunes shut himself away in strange isolation. Days went by without a single mass being said in Luar-do-Chão. The priest went out early in the morning and only returned at night. The sole faithful resident in the church was the donkey. The creature, with its silent wisdom, would never leave the church, becoming more of a practising Catholic than the regular churchgoers.

During this time, the priest prayed by himself on the bank of the River Madzimi. Grandma became a type of outdoor sacristan. She would take her plastic flowers there and stick them in the soil around the rock on which the priest knelt.

Once, Fulano Malta turned up in this isolated spot. Dulcineusa was very surprised. What was this wayward son of hers doing there? Fulano approached her, saying that he wanted to converse.

—*Confess?* asked the priest.

Yes, he could confess too, Fulano conceded. But he neither conversed nor confessed. He remained silent, serving as a chorus to Nunes's own silence. Sitting there, they both contemplated the river as if they were listening to things that only they were aware of. Until finally, my father decided to speak.

—*It was Mariavilhosa who was right.*

—*Right about what?*

—*We need to plant a baobab.*

—*A baobab? Where?*

—*In the river, Father. In the bed of the river. If we want to save the victims of the wreck, we've got to staunch the river's flow.*

Dulcineusa listened attentively for the priest's reply. She wanted to establish whether they were not both mad, both affected by the happenings and mishappenings on our Island. The priest didn't answer. He knew what Fulano was referring to. Nunes knew all about his story and that of his wife, Mariavilhosa. He knew how both their destinies were linked to the River Madzimi.

The priest still remembered how it had all begun between those two lovers, some thirty years before. One distant afternoon, the still young Fulano had joined the

crowd to await the arrival of the *Vasco da Gama*. Among
the sailors, he noticed the presence of a beautiful young
man with soulful eyes. Fulano was drawn to those eyes.
He found it strange that he was so attracted to the features
of a male like himself. It wasn't so much the eyes but the
look that the other devoted to him, which was furtive and
yet full of intention. Anxious at such an attraction, Fulano
asked himself whether he might not have fallen ill, whether
he wasn't indeed a sick man.

Contrary to his usual habits, Fulano Malta even went
to confession. Nunes listened in silence to his admission
of forbidden love. My father was obsessed: such a thing
couldn't be happening to him.

—*Father, am I normal?*

The priest's placating assurances were of no use. My
father's anguish grew along with his irrepressible passion.
On one occasion, he followed the sailor in order to ask
him for an explanation about something or other. All
this a mere pretext for tension and intention. The sailor
answered evasively, and asked that he should never address
him again. That he was a fugitive from the other shore, an
escapee from political persecution. He found it difficult
even to talk. The rigorous nature of his duties on the
ship had aggravated the physical weakness brought on
by his time in prison. Hence his fragile appearance, his
modest manner.

My father was taken aback. Such an excuse surrounded
the stranger with an extra layer of mystery. Fulano was
even more taken. The ship would arrive, and he would
stand there watching as it docked. And totally absorbed, he

would concentrate on the sailor's doleful, fragile gestures. One dark night, he followed the mariner along darkened paths, which led to the house of Amílcar Mascarenha. The doctor came to the door of his house, surveyed the street carefully, and then invited the sailor in.

Fulano crept into the undergrowth, infiltrating the shadows. From there he could see what was happening inside. The doctor told the sailor to take off his denim top. He could then see that his chest was swathed in a tight bandage. It must have been an extensive injury, such was the thickness of the bandage. Finally, when the cloth was unwound, Fulano Malta couldn't contain his surprise, for he saw two full breasts. The sailor, the enigmatic sailor, was after all a woman! Fulano Malta took a deep breath, so deep that he scarcely noticed himself burst into Mascarenha's house, taking the beautiful, half-clad woman by surprise. The girl didn't even attempt to cover herself. She came round the table, her eyes fixed on Fulano's, confronting him as if some new soul had come to her. Then, she covered herself with a capulana and left. Fulano sat down, bewildered at his discovery.

Then, the doctor told him the whole story: the girl was called Mariavilhosa. She lived further up the valley, on a part of the river that few people visited. Some months before, she had been visited by disaster: she had been raped and had become pregnant. In order to carry out a secret abortion, Mariavilhosa had used the root of the Lala palm. She had stuck it as deeply as she could in her uterus. When Mascarenha had found her, she was in a deplorable state: her insides were infected, her blood rotting in her womb.

He did what he could. But the girl would have to continue her treatment, and the only place this could be done was the capital. But at that time, blacks were forbidden to travel on the ship. The *Vasco da Gama* was for whites only. What did Mariavilhosa do? She disguised herself as a crew member. The only blacks allowed aboard were the sailors. She would be one of them, heaving ropes and turning winches. Fulano had met this fresh-water sailor and his heart had penetrated the disguise to seek out the woman of his life.

The story would have ended here were it not for the marks left on Mariavilhosa's body. The woman's womb had fallen permanently sick. And there was no possible medical cure. Whenever a child was born on the Island, blood seeped from the stitches and scars.

Mariavilhosa had had me in the middle of other frustrated attempts. But an anguish weighed her down like an anchor, preventing her from ever being happy. And this tortured me. It was as if I were an insufficient son, who had not been enough to fulfil her maternal needs. Even today, Mariavilhosa's melancholy left me depressed. Now that my grandmother was recalling it all, I took the opportunity to bring everything out into the open.

—*Is it true that my mother drowned?*

Drowned was just a way of saying. So had she committed suicide? Grandma chose her words carefully. It wasn't suicide either. What she did, one particular afternoon, was to wade into the river until she disappeared, swallowed up by the current. Had she died? People doubted it. Maybe she had turned into one of those water spirits who, years later, reappear with powers over the living. What's more, there was even someone who could testify that on that very afternoon, as Mariavilhosa waded into the river, she turned into water. When she disappeared into the river, she was already water. And nothing else but water. My father even jumped into the Madzimi in search of his beloved. He dived and swam backwards and forwards like some crazed porpoise. But something extraordinary happened: the moment he entered the water, he lost his sense of vision. He swam without seeing, here and there, bumping into tree trunks and running aground on the river bank. Until they made him give up and accept that sad state of unreality.

Grandpa Mariano wasn't the first, after all, to create family problems over funeral rituals. There wasn't even a body when my mother's funeral was being prepared. They ended up burying a vase full of river water.

—*Water is what she was, my dear grandson. Your mother is the river, she's flowing out there among those waves.*

To rediscover her original shape, it would be necessary to stop the flow of waters by planting baobab trees in the river's deep bed. And that task could only be done with the help of the gods. That's what folk said in Luar-do-Chão.

Dulcineusa's sigh was like a full stop at the end of a long narration. She rubbed her fingers together as if to show that she had finished turning the last page. She looked at me straight in the eyes and smiled:

—*Have you ever heard of such a thing? All this because of a donkey.*

—*And does Father know the whole story?*

—*What Fulano never found out was who raped Mariavilhosa.*

—*And who was it?*

—*I can't tell you.*

—*Tell me, Grandma, I need to know.*

Dulcineusa hesitated. I resorted to the infallible strategy of taking her hands and stroking her fingers.

—*Do you really need to know, my dear?*

—*I'm the one who is going to continue your line, Grandma. I need to know everything.*

—*It was Frederico Lopes, your godfather who received you when you went to the city.*

Lopes? Such a God-fearing man, such a good husband, getting involved with black women? It must be a mistake. Judging by his behaviour, no one would believe his guilt. But it was true. And known to Father Nunes. At that moment, my memory was suddenly illuminated: my mother's photo on Conceição Lopes's bedside table! The Portuguese woman had known what had happened between her husband and Mariavilhosa. And she was punishing Frederico by imposing the presence of my mother's face right next to the marital bed.

Father Nunes was aware of everything and couldn't forgive himself for absolving and re-absolving that man Lopes during Sunday confession. Just as he continued to absolve other younger dignitaries full of posture and possessions, but with blood on their criminal hands. Maybe it was to this tiredness that he was referring. Grandma had freed her fingers from mine and was talking slowly:

—*That's why I'm looking after that donkey brought in by the waters.*

—*I don't see the link, Grandma.*

—*That donkey isn't just an animal.*

—*But, Grandma, a donkey is a donkey.*

—*Let me tell you something, my dear: here in Luar-do-Chão we need a much purer angel. But the angel that stayed here would immediately lose all its purity. Perhaps you, my little Mariano...*

—*Perhaps what?*

—*Perhaps you are that angel.*

8   *The scent of an absent love*

> Those with most reason to weep
> are those who never weep.
> — *Father Nunes*

I walked down the corridor, my soul spiralling as if the
house were a womb and I were returning to my original
inner state. The bunch of keys that my grandmother had
given me jangled in my hand. They had already told me:
those keys weren't of any use whatsoever. They were for
old locks that had long been replaced. But Grandma
Dulcineusa kept them all because she suffered from one
particular belief: even if there was no door, the keys
prevented bad spirits from entering our abode.

I could now confirm that none of the keys fitted any
of the locks. All except for one in the loft, that opened
the door to the lumber room. I went into this dark space,
where there was no lighting, and a dank smell covered
everything like a sheet. I left the door half open in order to
leave a chink of light.

All of a sudden, the door closed. I was swallowed up
by the darkness at the same time as a body squeezed

me aggressively. I lost my balance, managed to regain it
and once again, the stranger threw himself at me. There
was no doubt in my mind: I was being attacked, they
were going to kill me once and for all, and I would be
buried before even Grandpa Mariano. All this flashed
through my head while I clumsily tried to defend myself.
I struggled, waved my arms and, when I tried to shout,
a hand covered my mouth, silencing me. The intruder
pressed up against my body until we were crushed, belly
to belly, and for the first time, I felt as if it was a woman.
Her breasts were stuck to my hands. Gradually, the
tense gestures grew weaker and out-and-out vigour was
converted into tenderness. It was no longer the hand that
covered my mouth, but lips, sweet, fleshy lips. Who was
it? I asked myself. The first person that occurred to me
was Aunt Admirança. Could it be? No. Admirança was
taller, fuller in body. The woman's hands were precise
in the way they unbuttoned me, leaving me ever less
dressed. At first, I resisted. I was bound by the prohibition
that I could not make love while in mourning. I even
managed to whisper:

—*We can't, there's a dead man...*

—*What dead man? Has someone died?*

The faceless woman bit my neck, giving me goose
spots. Her voice was indecipherable, heightened by
her breathlessness: soft, unclear, it insinuated itself and
gradually invaded my intimacy.

Everything happened vaguely, noiselessly, without
burden. Sex was never more delicious. For I was dreaming
my partner in love, dreaming of loving all women through

her. Admirança was the woman I would most like it to
have been. But this woman's flesh seemed to be of less
mature age. It must have been another, one of so many
guests who were frequenting the house. When it was over,
still gasping in the darkness, the woman placed a box in
my hands.

—*Give this to Abstinêncio.*

Then the shape disappeared beyond the door. I
could well have glanced down the hall to confirm my
suspicions. However, the desire to leave that woman's
identity in shadow was stronger. I had indeed made love,
in a void, to someone to whom I could give the face of
whoever I liked.

I left the house. I breathed the air like a new man,
putting behind me any memory of what had happened
in the lumber room. I had a clear mission: to find the
doctor. I needed to understand what was happening to
my grandfather. Amílcar Mascarenha was the man who
could best help me. When I asked after him in town, I
was told he was down at the shacks. That's where the
men of the Island would get together to drink, talk and
listen to music. The shacks were just round the corner,
everything is near in this place, just a few steps away. I
found Amílcar Mascarenha at the liquor store belonging
to the mulatto, Tuzébio. I asked him to accompany me,
but Amílcar refused. I was to sit down right there, while
he ordered me a large bottle of beer. Left with no other
choice, I sat down on an old crate, ignoring the chaos
all around.

Tuzébio waved to me, smiling, from behind the

counter. He pointed to the bottle of xidiba ndoba, the spirit that I used to come and fetch long ago, sent there by Grandpa Mariano.

—*The little bottle is waiting here!* Tuzébio announced.

—*Waiting?*

—*Waiting for your Grandpa to come back.*

The certainty on the bar owner's face almost pained me. So I got down to the business that had brought me there: I questioned the doctor on my grandfather's state. I wanted everything to be made clear to me, in a blaze of logic. I wanted to know whether my grandfather had suffered from some type of illness that might explain his end. Or better, his absence rather than his end. And while we were still unsure of what epilogue to write, what should we do: issue an interim death certificate? Finally, I wanted to know whether there was any rationale available in the textbooks of science to explain why Grandpa Mariano should be writing me letters.

The doctor didn't answer any of my questions: his gaze followed the girls that passed by. I realised that this was not the appropriate place, so I asked whether we could go somewhere else. The Goan agreed, but on one condition: that I should serve him some of that red wine we had at home, that fine Lisbon water he'd seen in the living room cupboard. I promised him he would have some. The doctor left the bar without paying.

And so Amílcar Mascarenha accompanied me along the dirty alleyways of the town. He was carrying with him an old briefcase that had once been of leather. The doctor paused by a ruined building. He was looking for something on the wall that time had peeled away. Amílcar was leaning over a stain that I couldn't make out.

—*Do you see?*

I came near and looked closely. There were the remains of some painted letters that were all but illegible: 'Down with the exploitation of man by man.'

—*I was the one who painted that!*

He was still proud, as if those letters were some artist's work. He shook his head and as he walked away, he kept looking back as if he were taking his leave of an epoch.

We passed by the church. Now, without Father Nunes, the building appeared fragile, vulnerable to the abuses of time and men. I asked the doctor to wait a moment for me. I went up the steps two at a time and when I reached the top I was almost knocked over by fright: a huge head appeared at the door. It was the donkey surveying the town, watching the world go by. The creature was chewing something. They were flowers. From inside, I could hear the unmistakable voice of my grandmother, Dulcineusa:

—*Come in, my dear grandson!*

I didn't go in. I peered through the half light and saw her carrying bundles of wild flowers. She looked back and pointed at the donkey:

—*I bring all these blooms to feed him.*

—*If no one gives him anything, he'll have to go outside, which is where he should be.*

Grandma received my comment with alarm. With her pelican's waddle, she came over and murmured in my ear:

—*Don't say such things, dear. I've already told you: this donkey isn't any old animal.*

Her voice tapered off even further until it was no more than a faint hiss. Obviously, she didn't want the donkey to hear:

—*That creature there has got a baptized soul.*

—*Come now, Grandma, you'll be telling me next he needs to go to confession...*

—*It's not a joking matter, Mariano.*

—*I'm talking seriously, Grandma.*

—*Remember one thing: all those folk who disappeared in the river are looking at us, right now, through the eyes of that creature. Don't forget that.*

She kissed me on the forehead and told me to go. I rejoined the doctor, who, in the meantime, had walked on down Middle Street. When we reached Nyumba-Kaya, we went straight to the room where visitors were received. I unleashed all my questions at once. Mascarenha didn't reply. He went over to the table where Grandpa was laid out. Almost automatically the Goan took the dead man's hand in his.

—*Can you feel his pulse?*

He didn't answer. With some sign of irritation, he opened his case and offered me his stethoscope.

—*Do you want to listen?*

—*I don't know how it works. I just want to know if he's alive.*

The Indian coughed, in order to give his pronouncement greater authority. According to him, there were signs of life, but they could only be grasped by the eyes of the soul, the secret windows of the spirit. Medical apparatuses were unable to read them.

—*Tell me something, doctor. If you had to decide, would you take him away for burial?*

—*It's a long time since I've had to decide anything at all. In fact that was the last decision I ever took.*

That was why he was here in Luar-do-Chão, tucked away in the periphery of the world. He had once been a revolutionary militant, he'd fought against colonialism and had spent years in prison. After Independence, he had been given positions of political responsibility. Then the revolution had ended and he lost all his jobs. He witnessed the death of the ideals that had given his life its sparkle. His race began to be pointed at and skin colour was gradually turned into an argument against him. Amílcar Mascarenha shut himself away in the Island and took refuge in drink. He gave free surgeries in his own home. His only piece of equipment was his tired old briefcase.

As I had promised, I went to the cupboard and plied him generously with wine. Amílcar looked at the glass closely and then focussed his gaze up above as if he had only just noticed that there was no ceiling. He began to savour his drink, his eyes closed like someone kissing. He passed his tongue over his lips to make sure that no drop was wasted. Only then did he address me. His tone was serious, and he seemed to have reassumed his medical posture: I should go and see Abstinêncio. He was the only person with the authority to delay the burial.

—*You were chosen by the dead man. But Abstinêncio is the eldest. He was the one chosen by life.*

He waved his empty glass, commenting on how clear

the glass was. It was his way of asking for more. I refilled his glass, while he reassured me: it was his last drink, his very last request. And I, saving time, replied:

—*I agree with you, doctor. I'll go and speak to my Uncle Abstinêncio. Please come with me!*

Before leaving, I went to get the box with which I had been entrusted in the lumber room. On our way to Uncle Abstinêncio's house, the Goan's spirits were already high, and he was more talkative than a crow in a coconut tree. My uncle was his only subject of conversation. He remembered Abstinêncio and laughed at the episodes that had filled their time together.

—*Do you know the story about the government office and the paint?*

Abstinêncio's life had been spent amid the stagnation of a government office. Everyone remembered the zealous public functionary: always the same shoulder leaning against the same doorpost. He and the building grew old together like brothers of the same age. One day, it was decided that the office should be painted and decorators assaulted walls, doors and windows with white paint. But they couldn't paint that piece of wood Abstinêncio leaned against. The man wasn't giving up his leaning post.

—*Only if they paint me along with it*, he insisted obstinately.

And so that piece of wall remained for ever after yet to be painted. As if it contained the portrait of that strange man's absence.

One recollection led to another. The doctor took pleasure in revealing episodes spent with my uncle. Did I

know, for instance, why he refused to leave his house? Did
I think he didn't love life? Well, it was the opposite: if my
uncle had shut himself away, refusing to go out, it wasn't
because he no longer loved his hometown. No, he loved
it so much that he didn't have the strength to watch it die.
When you walked through the town, what did you see?
Rubbish, more rubbish and yet more rubbish. And folk
living in the rubbish, off the rubbish, worth less than all
that muck together.

—*Never have we been more like animals.*

It wasn't so much the poverty that was destroying him.
Much more serious was the wealth that was germinating
goodness knows where and in what dark corners. And
the indifference of the powerful towards their brothers'
destitution. This was the hatred that was brewing in him
against Ultímio. My youngest uncle would visit the Island,
stiff-collared and full of starch. He and his luxurious
ways, belching his superior airs. He would come and go
without so much as an excuse me, all puffed up, like some
powerful animal.

—*He's one of those who think they're bigwigs just because
they're subject to the orders of new bosses.*

Sadly, the island folk were so humble that all they
wanted was to be like the great and the good. Most of them
envied all the lustre. But all he, Amílcar Mascarenha, saw
in Ultímio was the lowly, slithering worm. Deluded by his
volatile powers.

—*In the puddle where night is reflected, the toad fancies
he's flying among the stars.*

My father and Uncle Abstinêncio were enraged.

They directed towards Ultímio feelings that no brother should harbour.

—*We are not like that here on the Island. We are happy when someone in the family has some good luck and reaps the advantages of power.*

But it wasn't the case with our family. Neither Abstinêncio nor my father wanted any favours from that scoundrel Ultímio. His was hot money, it made your hands burn.

Abstinêncio was consumed by sadness. And by envy too. He was sad because of his brother Ultímio. And he was envious of his brother Fulano. He was distraught for not being courageous like his brother, who had embraced a cause, put on a uniform and fought against injustice. Abstinêncio was incapable of even dreaming of doing half the things that his brother Fulano had undertaken.

Little by little, our eldest uncle grew thinner, as if he wanted to insubstantiate himself. At first, the doctor suspected that there was some illness behind such skinniness. He had examined him. But he wasn't ill. Abstinêncio was thin through self-abasement: so as to be less visible.

For a time, he even believed that my uncle was losing his mind. For he changed his name. As if the one he had from baptism was no longer any use. My uncle took on the names of all those who died. When José died, he began to call himself José. When Raimundo passed away, he became Raimundo. When the doctor asked him the reason why he was hopping around from name to name, he replied:

—*It's because, like this, I think nobody's died.*

We arrived at Abstinêncio's house when daylight was already faltering. I was astonished to hear the sounds of a party wafting out of the house. The door was open, the living room in flagrant disorder, while half-dressed girls disported themselves in every corner. My eldest uncle greeted us in the hall, and he had changed so much that I almost didn't recognise him. He held out a bottle of beer for me:

—*Here, take it, there's plenty of drink for everyone. Then choose the girl you like the look of.*

—*There's no need, Uncle. I'm fine like this.*

—*Choose, my young nephew. For I never had the chance to choose.*

The girls, lots of them, exhibited themselves, while laughing loudly, as if laughter were a measure of their willingness. Some of them gestured to me invitingly. I was overcome with dizziness and I sat down to regain my wits. And I wondered to myself: so was Abstinêncio one person during the day and another at night? That image I had of him of constraint and reserve, his near saintliness, was evaporating before my disbelief.

The doctor walked up to my uncle, took his arm and propelled him towards a corner. He asked him to send the girls away and reimpose a semblance of order. Abstinêncio obeyed. He turned off the radio, clapped his hands and told the girls to leave. Gradually the house became peaceful once more. When at last we sat there in silence, none of us seemed to know what to say. In the end, I got up and gave him the cardboard box that I had brought from Nyumba-Kaya.

—*I brought you this, Uncle.*

He didn't open the box right away, but sat there with it on his knees. He took a deep breath, as if he was afraid of something. He was delaying, in his own mind, the arrival of this piece of news. He drew his knees together, straightened his back, and spoke in a whisper: here was the Uncle Abstinêncio I knew once more. He pointed at the disorder, the bottles all over the floor and asked me:

—*Are you surprised, my boy? Do you know why I do this sort of thing?*

—*I've no idea, Uncle.*

—*You went away from here, from Luar-do-Chão. Well, this is my way of leaving, do you understand?*

He was like a mountain, he continued. He had roots that ran deeper than the world. But sometimes he was skimmed by the wing of a dream – and his mind became disturbed. Getting drunk was his only emotional outlet. Drink gave him a brief moment when everything was new, to the extent that he felt fully alive again. Amílcar got to his feet to close the curtain, as if to put an end to the banter.

—*Why don't you open the box, Abstinêncio?*

Uncle pretended he hadn't heard the doctor. His hand on the lid of the box seemed to suggest an eternal postponement.

—*I know only too well the cause of the illness that puts you in this state,* Mascarenha insisted. —*It's love for a woman. That's your illness, Abstinêncio.*

I awaited Abstinêncio's embittered retort, a serene but vehement denial. But he didn't answer. Instead, he decided to open the box. And from it, he began to slowly pull out a long white dress. My uncle shivered, the gesture caused him to stutter and his eyes turned to liquid. He pulled the whole dress out of the box and placed it against his face. He inhaled his memory and sat there, his nose amongst its folds, as if he were drugging himself with perfumes of bygone times. Then he was overcome by a fit of convulsive sobbing, and it was as if his thinness were being shaken by a visitation from the spirits. The doctor made a sign for us to leave. We withdrew respectfully, without making a noise. We didn't even close the door so as not to interrupt the visit that Abstinêncio was receiving.

Once again we trudged along the town's narrow lanes, jumping over muddy puddles. My heart was burning with a sort of feeling akin to jealousy, and I was unable to keep my searing doubts to myself:

—*Memories of Admirança?*

—*Admirança?*

—*Yes, didn't that dress belong to my Aunt Admirança?*

The doctor burst out laughing. Admirança? No, the dress belonged to Maria da Conceição Lopes, the wife of the Portuguese trader. That was the reason for his time-honoured, accumulated melancholy. My uncle had once been enflamed by a more than forbidden love. A white woman, the wife of a man of rank, one of the leading men of the Island.

I smiled out of surprise at such a revelation. Dona Conceição? So was that, after all, the reason behind my godmother's endless yearning? All those countless times she caught the boat to return to Luar-do-Chão were so that she could visit my solitary uncle! And I had never been aware. Only now could I understand why Abstinêncio had come to see me off when I had left the island some ten years before. The man had taken his time hugging me, overflowing with anticipated longing. But it wasn't me he was hugging. Through me, he was saying farewell to the woman accompanying me, the esteemed wife of Lopes, the boss.

9 *The kiss of the dead man in his slumber*

The good thing about the road
is that there's a way back.
Time is the only one-way journey.
— *Curozero Muando*

I woke up in the middle of the night. I seemed to hear a
noise. I fancied I saw a figure through the darkness. I got
up, searched the room, but there was no one. Maybe it was
the curtain, ruffled by the wind. Ever since the incident
in the lumber room, I ardently hoped for a second visit
by that anonymous woman. I wanted her once again to
unpack my desires amid groans and sweat.

I lit the candle and saw a paper fluttering on the
floor. Another letter? I leaned over and read. This time,
it was no more than a brief note. Finished abruptly as if
its mysterious author had been obliged to interrupt his
writing. The laconic text read as follows:

*Mariano, this is your urgent task: don't let them
go ahead with the burial. Once the ceremony is*

finished, you will no longer receive any revelations.
And without these revelations, you will be unable
to complete your mission to placate the spirits
with angels, God with the gods. These letters are a
way of teaching you what you must know. In this
case, I can't use traditional methods. You are now
far removed from the Malilanes and their magic
powers. Writing is the bridge between our spirits
and theirs. A first bridge between the Malilanes and
the Marianos.

Some members of the family will want to curtail
this moment. They will impose their own schedule
upon our time. Don't allow this to happen. Don't
allow it. Your task is to put lives back together
again, and straighten out the destinies of our people.
Each one has his secrets, his conflicts. I shall leave
you advice on how to conduct the affairs of your
relatives. It won't only be through letters. I shall
visit you in your dreams as well. In order that you
should know the inner feelings of your family. And
everyone here is a member of your family. Or at least
they are familiarised. Your father with his bitterness,
his crippled dream. Abstinêncio with his fears, bound
so tightly to his ghosts. Ultímio who doesn't know
where he comes from and only respects powerful
people. Your Aunt Admirança whose cheerfulness is
no more than a lie. Dulcineusa with her ravings,
poor soul. But one thing I ask of you is to begin with
Miserinha. Go and look for Miserinha. Bring this
woman to Nyumba-Kaya. These walls are growing

yellow with yearning for the woman. She should belong to us again. She's our family. And family is not something that exists in bits and pieces. It's all or it's nothing.

I examined the paper from top to bottom. Who was writing these notes? Could it be my father? But as far as I knew, my father had never even written his signature completely. Abstinêncio? Maybe, but why would he resort to such an enigmatic form of communication? Admirança was a woman for talking, face to face. She wouldn't hide behind calligraphy. My suspicions were directed mainly towards Dito Mariano. The probable, in this case, lay in the impossible. Did my grandfather awaken from his sleep-like state, climb the stairs and busy himself with writing to me?

I left the room, and made my way down the hall, looking for signs of our unknown house-breaking scribe. Silence. Suddenly, there were sounds coming from the room where the dead man was laid out. All of a shiver, I was paralysed by fear. I peered through the half-light in the manner of cats that scrutinise the darkness at the dead of night.

That was when I saw Grandma Dulcineusa, all stealth, furtively entering the room. She was wearing the clothes of bygone times, ceremonious laces that brushed along the floor. And then she displayed herself, hands on hips, before the dying man. All of a sudden, she began to dance, her large body swaying against the swirl of her skirts. I drew nearer under cover of darkness. Dulcineusa stopped dancing, as if somewhere, in some imaginary place, the music had come to a stop. Had she noticed me? But once again, she began to rock, and little by little, her dance turned into foreplay. Grandma Dulcineusa bent over the dead man's corpse, and passed her fingers affectionately over his face, while openly displaying her cleavage.

—*It's hot in here, my dear husband.*

She began to unbutton his jacket, while running her hand down his shirt. What was happening? Did my grandmother want to make love to the dead man? I felt guilty at being there, peeping at someone else's intimacy. Then Dulcineusa's voice took me by surprise.

—*You rogue, Mariano.*

Was she addressing me? She repeated: you're a hell of a rogue, Mariano. My heart shrank with anxiety. But no. Dulcineusa was talking to the original Mariano, her former husband. She sat down on the edge of the table and took out balls of thread and a needle from a little bag.

—*Mariano, be careful, I'm going to sew the button back on to your trousers.*

Her hands went to work on the dead man's flies. Dulcineusa later confessed to me that that was how her husband liked to begin their intimate dealings. One of them pretending it was something else, like the cat that looks away in distraction while clutching its prey in its claws. Such was this tacit agreement between them: he would arrive home and pretend one of his buttons was coming off. Dulcineusa would arm herself with her sewing gear and would position herself in order to measure and pleasure him. Then her needle would come and go dangerously, while her husband would close his eyes, absorbed in the pleasures that grew more bulky by the second.

She was now repeating this ritual. Grandma would begin her darning, imitating the movements of a professional seamstress. And in the meantime, she would embark on small talk:

—*Your grandson, Mariano, confessed your secrets to me. Yes indeed, that you loved me after all. Don't move as I might hurt you… Yes, he said you loved me more than all the others. That's why I came down here, now that there's no one about, and I was missing you so much.*

On and on went the confessions, trotted off in a dull tone of voice. Picked off like rosary beads, some of them escaped me here and there. For as she went on, she withdrew more and more into herself. She made to cut the thread with her own teeth, and took the opportunity to lean even further over Mariano's body. All I could hear of her speech was a muffled litany. But I managed to hear what she was asking for: a first night again, another chance for her to display her nudity to him for the very first time. So many times had she come to his bed in a state of undress. But never naked.

—*Yes, Mariano, now I shall be both unclothed and naked, at the whim of your hands.*

What she remembered most clearly of Mariano: his hands. There was nothing more tangible than those hands, a man's hands upon a woman's body. She could feel herself quiver as if she were changing her state, as if she were about to be reshaped. His hands melted her, fire turning iron into liquid form. As if her heart were being consumed

by the very hollowness of her chest, as if night were
shrinking the moon.

Lulled by my grandmother's confessions, I allowed
languidness to take over, and I slumped against the
cupboard behind which I was hiding. Dulcineusa got
a fright. With her oil lamp, she did the rounds of the
furniture. Until she saw me.

—*Is that you, Mariano?*

—*I'm sorry, Grandma.*

—*Why did you frighten me?*

I explained, all at sixes and sevens. I was expecting to
receive a vigorous reprimand from her. But she believed
she owed me more of an explanation.

This is what she had planned: in order to confirm
whether her husband was really dead, she would go down
to the parlour. She would provoke Dito Mariano, seduce
him with her mouth-watering stitches. She would wear
the oldest and most extravagant of her dresses, the ones
that he liked so much. She would douse herself in the
scents and perfumes that he had loved to sniff. And in this
way, she would find out whether it was a case of final and
irreversible decease.

—*So have you reached a conclusion?*

—*Almost. Yes, almost.*

—*Hasn't Grandpa reacted at all? Not even a tiny bit?*

—*Not even the tiniest of tiny bits.*

She shook her head decisively: her man was stone dead.
I trembled at the firmness with which she put paid to the
matter. Grandma shouldn't be so sure of herself. It would
only need one word from her and all their hopes would

be shattered, while Dito Mariano would sink into the darkness of the soil. I resorted to something that I knew she held sacred.

—*I also have a confession to make. Take a look at these papers…*

I took the letters out of my pocket and held them out for her to see. Dulcineusa took a step back in horror. Those were not things one should touch with one's hands. As she refused to cast her eyes over the papers, I ended up telling her the story of the sheets of paper that had appeared and their mystery. She remained silent, her eyes wide open in her dark face.

—*Show me those papers again…*

She brought the lamp nearer. She seemed to want to flood the suspicious letters with light. But then she allowed the flame to touch the sheet, and in no time at all, the paper had been consumed.

—*Grandma, you've burned the letters!*

—*Those letters, my dear grandson, those letters could only have brought disaster.*

I took her hands, softening her heart. I caressed her fingers, even over her scars, as if trying to correct her past. Her sigh gave me courage:

—*Grandma, I want to ask you something.*

—*What is it, Grandson?*

—*Don't let them bury Grandpa just yet.*

—*But why? We can't leave him there for the flies.*

—*But what if he's alive? Have you thought what a crime we'd be committing if he's alive?*

—*I don't know, dear. God will tell us what we've got to do.*

—*Some people will insist on our hurrying up the funeral. Don't allow that to happen, Grandma.*

She remained without speaking, stirring the ashes and the remains of the paper. She looked as if she had nothing more to do than to read her husband's words. I knew I shouldn't interrupt her at this solemn moment, but I was scared Grandma might suffer one of her absences of mind. And so I fired a question at point-blank range:

—*Who is Miserinha, Grandma?*

—*Miserinha? Who told you about that woman?*

—*I travelled here with her, we were on the same boat.*

—*And why on earth do you want to know about her?*

—*She forgot her scarf and I want to give it to her...*

—*You don't know how to lie, my dear. Tell me something: was that woman's name mentioned in the papers that I burned?*

—*Yes, Grandma.*

Once again, Dulcineusa sighed as if she feared something irreparable were happening. She blew the dust off her hands and looked up at the air as if it were powdered time that was falling to the ground. Finally, she murmured:

—*Miserinha is my sister-in-law.*

The fat Miserinha had been married to a brother of Dulcineusa, the late Jorojo Filimone. When her husband died, relatives turned up that Miserinha had never seen before. They took everything from her, her effects, her land. Even the house. It was after this that she resurrected the name of Miserinha, which had been given her when she was a teenager.

In the manner of the tradition in Luar-do-Chão, Dito

Mariano had regarded it as his mission to look after the widow. But it never happened. Grandma had opposed it tooth and nail. So they had moved her to a little hovel with only one room. And there she had remained, scarcely caring for herself. Miserinha had partially lost her sight as a result of an accident that she didn't want to tell anyone about. Nor did she ever openly accept her deficiency. Her vision grew still dimmer as she went on living in the hut. During the journey on the boat, she had told me she couldn't see colours. But the only thing fat little Miserinha could see were shadows. And voices.

—*Do you want to find Miserinha? Go to the market, my dear. She's in the habit of sleeping there, amid the banter of the stallholders.*

She put the needle and thread away in her sewing box. With a silent gesture, she summoned me near to her.

—*These letters, I got one too. I decided to burn it right away. To get rid of all trace of it.*

—*What did the letter say, Grandma?*

—*It talked of my sister-in-law. That we should bring her back to the house. It was a state of affairs that your grandfather never accepted, and now he's taken it with him...*

—*And do you agree, Grandma?*

—*It's stubbornness, my dear. I've never in my life had to agree or disagree. And I'm not going to learn now.*

—*So what shall we do, Grandma?*

—*Bring this woman Miserinha back with you.*

—*But will she come? Do you think she'll agree?*

—*Tell her to come and see the deceased.*

Once again I took my leave. I touched her on the

shoulder by way of a caress. She seized my arm and whispered:

—*Your grandfather isn't completely dead. I lied to you about his state a minute ago. I saw...*

—*What did you see?*

—*While I was sewing the button back on his trousers, I felt him.*

—*You felt...?*

—*I felt that he could feel me.*

10 Shadows of a world without light

When I was single, I cried.
When I was married, I had
nothing left to weep.
When I was a widow, tears
felt a yearning for me.
— *Miserinha*

The following morning, I left early for the fish market in
search of Miserinha. I remembered her from the deck
of the boat that brought me to Luar-do-Chão. I seemed
predestined to meet the fat lady again. The scarf she had
thrown into the waters of the river still floated in my gaze.
For my protection, she had said.

In the market, I went rummaging around among the
vegetables and the stalls where women sold fish. There was
a heaving mass of people, for you could find everything
there, from needles to truck chassis. Youngsters rolling
pieces of sugar cane between their teeth brought back tastes
of old to me. I remembered the crowds in the city and how
my father described them: *there are only two types of people:
some come up to us to ask for money, the others to rob us.*

At last I caught sight of Miserinha. There she was, half asleep, talking with the market women.

—*Miserinha?*

—*That's almost me, Miserinha Botão.*

She didn't look at me. She was concentrating on measuring my voice. Finally, she exclaimed:

—*Is that you, my nephew?*

Then she launched herself forward, without much direction, to give me a hug. Her arms lingered around me, while she whispered in my ear: we were family, she knew it ever since she saw me on the boat. Sharper than a razor, life had severed the links between our lives. But time then fancies itself as a stitcher. She had remembered my voice from the moment she had recognised me during our crossing of the river.

—*Aunt Miserinha, Grandpa wants you to come to our house.*

—*I know, he always did. But I can't.*

—*But it's your home.*

—*My home is this whole world. Here and the other side of the river.*

Her refusal was final. I couldn't understand. Miserinha explained: nowadays, everything was sand without any castle. There was a place to reside and there was a place to live. What she needed now was a place to die. She asked me to hear her simple request: as long as I was on the Island, I was to take a stroll along the back streets just to make sure she hadn't collapsed in some dark alley.

This was her greatest fear: to be left like those poor wretches who die and are left along the roadside to rot, without love or respect. This turning our back on people had never happened before. In Luar-do-Chão, there wasn't even a word for 'poor'. The term used was 'orphan'. But this was real poverty: not to have a family. Miserinha exclaimed: how ill we are, all of us! Was it she who was seeing shadows? Or was it all the rest of us who couldn't see anything, sightless for having ceased to see other people's suffering?

—*That's why I've become like an animal, rummaging around among the dust.*

She had learned to live in the to-and-fro between the city and the Island. She sought solidarity among the throngs of travellers, as if a crowd were one united body that helped her on her way. The boat made her feel younger, she said.

—*No Christ ever walked on those waters.*

Her life had passed just like the wind that blows against us, returning our spittle to our faces. In the city, it was easy to forget. For she joined the multitude of beggars and wandered the great avenues. She would beg from the whites. And the Indians. It's sad to be at the whim of another race in order to survive, Miserinha would say. But in the end, family doesn't depend on blood, or race. Whose kin are we? She would ask. Not even the poor join together now in solidarity.

—*Sometimes I get things given me, bits of money. I was given that scarf, the one that fell into the sea.*

From a fold in her capulana, she produced some coins that she had. She counted them, more by the sound they made than by their shape. She had developed that skill in which the poor and the rich seem to be alike – they only know how to count when it's a question of money.

—*Miserinha, we want you to live in our house.*

—*Is Admirança there?*

—*Yes, she is. Why?*

There was a sad smile, an imperceptible grunt. Relief is the twin of disappointment. Both express themselves in the same way: by means of a sigh. And it was with a sigh that Miserinha added:

—*I can't go to Nyumba-Kaya. For that house no longer has a root. Before long it will be gone.*

—*Gone?*

—*They're going to take the house away, my little one.*

—*How?*

—*They're going to take everything. They've already taken our soul. Now, all that's left is the Island.*

She signalled me to leave. She had her chores to do, her secret obligations. If she could no longer see, she had that tiny satisfaction of keeping part of her daily existence hidden. I was to leave her alone, for it was time for her to set off along paths to nowhere in particular, paths measured only by the depth of their shadows.

I respected her request and returned to Nyumba-Kaya. Without thinking, I burst into the reception room. There was Grandpa, persistent in his horizontality. I stood there next to his body, in solitary vigil. I was afflicted by an absurd desire to lie down on the floor and look up at the heavens, with only Dito Mariano for company. So that's what I did. Lying flat on the ground, I was able to enjoy the peace and quiet, and almost fell asleep. The absence of a roof as I looked up suggested a chimney, from which clouds emerged. And thus languid, I fell asleep.

I woke up, shaken by the shock of no longer feeling the ground. Moreover, I didn't know where I was. I looked around, baffled, and even fancied I saw Grandpa's leg move. There was a sheet on the ground next to me. My chest was heaving as I lifted a corner of the cloth. As if trying not to awaken a sleeping child, I then noticed that the sheet covered some papers. I grabbed them, trembling. The same handwriting, the same challenge to my astonished eyes:

Didn't I ask you? Didn't I ask you not to reveal how I make my apparitions? Why did you show those letters to Dulcineusa? You broke your promise. The only thing left for me to do now is to declare myself, and lose my ultimate mystery. I, your grandfather, Mariano, am the one speaking to you through these letters. Don't ask any more questions, don't have any more doubts. It is I, Dito Mariano, who am your shadowy correspondent.

Why do I write? Why don't I make a voicely apparition, addressing you from inside your head? I write to you so as to increase the distance between us. I could talk to you as you peer up into the roofless room. But my voice is no longer visible. And besides, I have one fear: that I may breathe my last sigh next to you. You would then run the risk of accompanying me into this chasm. So I use your hand, your calligraphy, to explain my motives. I'm like the maybug. I open my wings, the outer ones, in order

*to merely hover. For deep inside, hidden away, are
the other wings, the real flyers, the ones that take me
away from myself.*

*Have you heard Dulcineusa talking about me?
Such yearning, my God, so much longing devoted to
me. I even feel sorry for myself, for only now does
she reveal the extent of her love for me. Poor thing,
she loved me so much. But what can I say about
love? She wanted proof of it and I, out of respect
for tradition, couldn't demonstrate my love for a
woman. Over there, in the city, I've heard you've
now adopted the ways of whites. And you hold
hands and even kiss each other in public. But here,
only a man who has been bewitched demonstrates his
affection for a woman.*

*Old age has taught me something: love is the
domain of those who are alive. Or maybe love is
the mother of all living things. But I, even before,
was never truly alive. That's why love was never
really for me.*

*Nor do I even know what drew me to
Dulcineusa, but it was as if I could guess that I
would eventually die in her arms. Dulcineusa
was the woman who saw me off. I had so often
abandoned myself inside her body. And it was inside
that very body that I would take leave of my own
self. As if she had become my mother and I were
descending through her body like a maternal sigh.
Thus was my posthumous parturition.*

Now they want to pack me off to the cemetery.

Before, I wouldn't have minded. I would linger there, among those trees so full of shade. The cemetery was so pretty, so restful that it even made you feel like dying. In those days, a little stream ran through it, a thread of water as slender as a young girl. I would look at the graves, all lined up for eternity, and I would want to sleep. All this happened when I was a young lad and life wasn't painful yet. But now, I avoid the place, keep away from it.

Dulcineusa knows all about these likes and dislikes, just as she knows everything about me. Did you see how she shook at the sound of Miserinha's name? That's because the woman was my mistress for many years. Dulcineusa knew about it from the beginning. I don't care, she would say. Even though it was my duty to look after Miserinha, in accordance with tradition. These are ancient dictates, which we can accommodate. That's what Dulcineusa said. But what was true for the mouth wasn't for the heart. Deep down, she was jealous to the point of wishing death upon her sister-in-law. Miserinha knows of her hatred. That's why she refuses to come. And who knows, maybe she's got used to living along the shadowy edges of life's path. It's therefore best that these women are left to live separately. Each one contemplating their private yearning. What you should do is to visit the gravedigger, Curozero Muando. He'll explain the secrets of our world to you.

Mariano

PS Now I have a special request: bring me a tasty young girl, firm of flesh, for me to hold during my final moment. So that, at that very point in time, I can indulge myself in the illusion that I am not dissolving into nothingness all by myself.

I put the letter down with a snigger: a young girl to complete his farewell? Grandpa wanted to die like a fish, with its body in its mouth. I peered at the supposed corpse. I gave voice to my anxieties out loud:

—*No, Grandpa, it can't be you, sir, who wrote this.*

—*Grandson: are you praying there next to your grandfather?*

It was my grandmother, Dulcineusa, interrupting me. Against the light, I found it easier to distinguish her voice than her shape. Grandma advanced, sure of foot, and took the paper from my hand.

—*Give me that piece of filth!*

She tore the letter up. And she followed this by ripping the pieces that remained. With every tear, each snip of paper contained no more than a word. The little pieces fell from her fingers and fluttered around near the ground.

—*Grandma, why did you tear something up that wasn't even yours?*

—*Quiet, Grandson. Show some respect for I have some guests coming.*

Then, turning towards the door, she summoned someone in whom I didn't recognise immediately. But then, from the indecisive dragging of her feet, I guessed that it must be the corpulent Miserinha. Grandma pulled her along by the arm with open pride, as if she was exhibiting a trophy of war.

—*Are you surprised, dear Grandson? Well, it was I who brought my sister-in-law here. She's going to stay here with me.*

With her blinking eyes, Miserinha surveyed the room as if she were capturing invisible beings. She held Dulcineusa with both hands while she murmured:

—*Lead me, sister. Lead me to where he is!*

The two women advanced with difficulty towards the funeral table. Then Grandma stepped back in silence. Miserinha stood there alone before the dead man. And there she lingered. Without uttering a word or making a single gesture. Finally, with a sigh, she said with uncertain voice:

—*This man's a liar! He's lying, just as he always does.*

11 Searing doubts sizzling women

Here's the difference:
those who once died of hunger,
now die from lack of food.
— *Tuzébio, the bar owner*

—*Mariano! Marianooo! Come here, Mariano!*
   This was the voice of the womenfolk back in the old days, during my childhood. They would call me to light the stove. They were observing an ancient precept: only a man could light a fire. Women had the task of drawing water. And so eternal values were repeated: fire and water warmed to each other in the kitchen, stoked by a woman's gesture. Just as in the heavens, the gods welded rain and lightning flash.
   The kitchen transported me back to distant savours. As if, amidst the opaqueness of its vapours, it wasn't food that was being prepared, but time itself. It was on the kitchen floor that I invented toys and scratched my first drawings. It was there that I listened to voices talking and laughing, and the swish of skirts. It was there that I was given the flavours of my upbringing.

It wasn't just the house that marked us off as different in Luar-do-Chão. Our kitchen was unlike the others. In the Island, the kitchens are outside, out in the back yards, separated from the rest of the house. But we lived in the European style, cooking inside, and eating behind closed doors. In the beginning, there was some resistance to this. I remember how my grandmother would carry the pots and pans outside and then back inside again. Other women would pass by balancing cans of water on their head, as if they were listening to the rhythm of the earth under their bare feet. And the mesh door, sluggishly banging time and again against the jamb. The mortar remained faithfully on the ground. And the thump-thump as the women ground the corn in it. I used to especially like watching Aunt Admirança pitching her body against the grains.

It was she who was now grinding the corn. In ceremonies for the dead, the living have to be given sustenance. And it seems that appetites get larger when in the presence of the deceased. I offered to help her, but she just smiled: men aren't supposed to get involved with the pestle. It was enough for me to stand there watching, that was help enough. Sweat soaked her brow, and drops fell into the corn. Good, I thought, the food will taste of her. Her hand tidied a lock of hair, as if there were a way of controlling those tresses. Then, with an undulating movement of her body, she bent over, emphasising her voluptuousness.

My aunt was a woman of mystery, with some parts of her life an incomplete narration. She had been away before

I was born. Not far away, but it was on the other shore, the other side of the river. And that was enough for us not to know anything about her. What sort of a country is it where someone moves just a short distance away, and yet it's on the other side of the world? Admirança only returned years later, when my eyes were old enough to savour life a little.

Admirança suffered the heaviest burden that can befall a woman on this side of the world: she was sterile. It was said that her blood had not blossomed. Our aunt preferred to avoid the subject.

—*I'm entering free motherhood, now this one's mother, now that one's. I do short-term mothering. For example, at the moment I'm Miserinha's mother.*

It wasn't without reason that she was keeping an eye on Miserinha. She received alarming tales of Miserinha's craziness. Folk said, for instance, that she was eating bits of glass. She believed that by swallowing such splinters, she would become transparent. Admirança made allowances for everything, excusing Miserinha by saying:

—*That woman has suffered misfortunes that only I know about.*

Love had castigated her, life hadn't offered her any gifts. Love has a habit of punishing us so gently that we believe we are being caressed. Miserinha had lost her husband, Jorojo, but hadn't gained her lover, Mariano. Now, the tubby old lady was little more than a shadow, accommodated in a back room. There, she invented her clothes and indulged in her daydreams. Admirança mothered her, condescendingly.

—*I'm mother to all this, the house, the family, the Island.
And I can even be mother to you, Mariano.*

Her laughter couldn't disguise a trace of sadness. Deep
down, she knew that with old Mariano's disappearance, the
foundations of all her certainties were turning to clay. She
could foresee the demise of the family, the dissolution of
the house, the passing of the land.

—*When old Mariano disappears, what is going to keep
us together?*

I patted her cheek, to chase away her despair. I had
rarely seen her so openly anxious.

—*Aunt, I want to thank you very much.*

—*Thank me for what, nephew?*

—*For never showing your sadness. You give off so many
smiles, Aunt, that you seem such a happy person, always
so happy.*

—*I'm like a winged ant, see?*

The winged ant only has one flight in its life. After
this brief journey, its wings fall off, two little fragments
of transparency that no longer have a use. It collapses on
to the ground in order to become a queen. That's how
Admirança felt: she had enjoyed her little piece of sky. And
she returned to her pestle, her vigorous gestures no longer
grinding corn, but sad memories.

I went back into the kitchen and sat down next to the
table. Grandma Dulcineusa sang her ditties while keeping a
watch on the saucepan over its low flame. I fell into a deep
sleep. When I awoke I was alone, having lost all sense of
time. The first thing I saw was the letter. It was resting on
a plate. As I reached out to take it, I knocked over a glass.

In an instant, the paper was flooded by the water. I read it quickly before the letters dissolved and the ink faded.

My dear Grandson, I see you're going around trying to find out how I died. Do you want to know how my illness started? The truth is that I don't know yet. Does an illness have a beginning? Or is it like love: these things only exist after we've remembered them? Who knows whether my illness didn't begin even before it happened? I wasn't suffering from any definite symptom when I went to the hospital and saw Doctor Amílcar Mascarenha. I wasn't suffering any pain but I was anxious to be cured. What was I complaining of? I didn't know. Maybe I complained about my sleep, which was so light that it scarcely touched me. I was sleeping badly, it had always been like that. The only time I slept was when there was no such thing as time: in my mother's womb.

It wasn't a valid complaint? So I said: wait, doctor, don't send me away for I need to listen to your words. Merely hearing certainties like the ones you utter is like a beach under the foot of a shipwrecked sailor. So what illness did he recommend for me, given that I had failed to come up with an appropriate one of my own? Mascarenha was scared of prescribing me an illness. So I encouraged him: doctor, don't be afraid to speak. Assign me an illness, even if it's only a dose of women's fever. To be honest, I'd prefer that. A woman, doctor, a woman doesn't

need to turn herself into a child in order to be happy.
But we men, we find it difficult to be joyful. In order
to laugh heartily, our power of judgement needs to
shrink. Assign me a woman's illness. Give me one of
their intimate bits to malfunction, for their insides
are so full of such organs.

At that point, the doctor didn't want to waste
time talking to me. Time counted, for him, and had
its cost. He got up and paced up and down his office,
observing the floor, as if in meditation. He wasn't
meditating, but measuring the traces of mud that my
shoes had left behind in my slovenliness. I'm sorry,
doctor, that's the way my feet behave. It's because I've
come out of the mud, wet dust. It's this rain, and I
pointed through the window, this rain that doesn't
stop, so much so that there's almost no sky left. I
confessed a secret to him at that moment: rain causes
me to become cleverer. There are things I can only see
through raindrops, on a rainy day. You, sir, I said
to Amílcar Mascarenha, you studied in books and
overseas. Am I right, doctor? Wasn't it abroad that
you studied? That's all very well, but it's not right.
Books are foreign as far as I'm concerned. For I study
through the rain. It's the rain that's my teacher.

The doctor listened to all this without
interrupting me. And for me, his listening almost
cured me. So then I said, I've had my course of
treatment. It was thanks to the time you gave me,
doctor. That's what I haven't had enough of in my
life: people agreeing to listen to me, lending an ear to

my confessions. Take my wife, who spends her time talking to God. And I'm left, reduced to silence. Even on Sunday mornings, I remain silent. And in my silence, I begin to pray. For people pray better when they don't know they're praying. Silence, doctor, silence is the language of God.

It was silence that helped me when I visited my cousin, Carlito Araldito, a cobbler by trade. I would sit down and watch him at work. When I left, I would say: you know, Araldito, my life is like one of those shoes that have become worn thin through age. You can put it back on, the leather can be made to shine again, but we are the ones who can no longer shine. Do you understand? As if we were second-hand. Or in this case, second-foot. We would laugh, but without really feeling like it. Me and Araldito. We would talk about ourselves as if we were talking about friends who had died. We were attending our own funeral.

Signed and witnessed: Dito Mariano

There in the solitude of the kitchen, I read it while the letters faded on the damp paper. Then, all that was left was a limp sheet of paper on which the writing had lost all its shape and memory. I remain absorbed within myself, unaware of time, whenever I listen to voices. There were people in the parlour. I went to have a look. It was Uncle Ultimio pacing up and down between the four walls. He didn't notice me there. What was he doing? He was talking, engaged in conversation with Grandpa. His tone was stern, almost threatening. I confronted him, moved by a mischievous urge:

—*Are you talking to Grandpa, Uncle Ultímio?*

He was taken by surprise and took time before answering. Talking to the deceased? Who, him? He was talking to himself, in secret, behind closed mouth. Ultímio stammered while he walked round the table. He passed his hands over the walls, collecting paint that had begun to flake in the damp air.

—*See what they've done? These folk destroy, wipe out everything. Who told them to take the wretched roof off?*

Ultímio knew that it was tradition that dictated this. But he couldn't accept that I, formed and educated in the city, should not have opposed it. As far as he was concerned, the practice was obsolete. Other values were accumulating within him.

—*Like this, the property loses its value...*

Then, he confessed the extent of his ambition. He wanted to get rid of the family house. Sell Nyumba-Kaya to foreign investors. A hotel would be built on the site.

—*But, Uncle, this house...*

—*Only the past lives here. Why should we hang on to this dump now that Grandpa has died? Quite apart from anything else, the Island has a great future. You don't know it yet, but things are going to change big time round here...*

I resisted him, presenting counter-arguments against his charges. Nyumba-Kaya couldn't be allowed out of our hands, to be removed from our lives. Ultímio laughed. For him, I was no more than the kid he'd always known.

To cap things, I still refused his invitations to become the administrator of his business dealings.

—*The problem is the old man who won't be on his way. And that doctor who can't make up his mind.*

—*It's not a decision for the doctor...*

—*Yes, but what is that man Mascarenha saying? The old man is either dead or he's still clinically...*

—*Mascarenha is consistent in what he has said from the beginning.*

—*I don't trust that Indian guy. I'm going to send for a black doctor. A doctor of our own race, I don't want a bunch of Indians interfering...*

—*You can't decide things by yourself, Uncle Ultímio.*

—*But I'm the one paying for things by myself. Or is someone else going to pay?*

And on he ranted. He couldn't understand his brothers: on the one hand, they obeyed tradition to the point of destroying that dirty old roof; on the other, they placed their faith in a doctor's opinion. And an Indian one, to make matters worse. I smiled incredulously. I knew that Ultímio had business dealings with Indians and had grown rich through investments in land with those he now referred to derogatorily as 'monhês'. In some matters, race was important, in others, not. That's what I felt like saying, but didn't have the courage.

—*Come with me, let's go for a spin!* my uncle ordered.

He wanted some company on a drive round the Island. He wanted to show me the tracts of land where he intended to make money. Above all, he wanted to show me his car, that four-wheel drive full of shiny metal fittings.

—*I'm not having any more sons-of-bitches laying a finger on this!*

He'd sent for new tyres and windows from the city. I accepted, almost out of laziness. My heart was torn by a deep sense of sadness: I watched the house receding through the car window. Until it faded into the mist. Ultímio was far removed from my sad thoughts. He was too busy explaining the value of his car, which had just been launched on to the African market.

—*I'm prepared to bet there isn't another car like this in the country. Mine's the only one.*

Uncle Ultímio intended to hold on to his land holdings, and even wanted to establish a casino on the Island, in the middle of a huge expanse of terrain.

—*But there are people living here!*

—*People? Oh, those...*

—*What are you going to do with them?*

—*We'll have to see, we'll have to see. Everything will be done legally, in conformity with the law. For the time being, I'm going to put the properties in my wife's name. You remember her, don't you?*

—*Of course I remember. I even know that she's not in the country.*

—*She went to visit the kids and to stay over there for a bit.*

His relationship with his wife had been an embittered one for some time. But the newly rich followed the age-old precept: you don't leave your wife. The husband gets himself new girlfriends, that's true, as many as the number of apartments he rents in different parts of the city. I had been told about all this discord, but I wasn't the type to spread it around. I was also told that Ultímio was very thin, and there was a fear he might be ill. But there was no evidence of that: Uncle was looking sleek and prosperous. He knew I was looking at him, and he patted his stomach as he interrogated me.

—*Do you think I've put on weight, nephew? Do you think I've got a tycoon's paunch?*

—*I haven't said anything, Uncle.*

—*You're wrong, Mariano: it's the poor who grow the fattest.*

We arrived at the cemetery, and he stopped the engine. His tone of voice denoted a serious turn in the conversation: he had brought me there to convince me to share his opinions during family meetings. We needed to be of one voice. So as to settle the dispute and move on to practical matters. He was the one who knew the way forward, he was the one who had power and influence.

—*Grandpa was senile when he nominated you, a mere kid…*

Uncle didn't wait for an answer from me. Suddenly, he turned his back, got out of the car and crept off between two walls. What was he going to do? I wondered. After little more than a minute, he returned leading a young woman. She was possibly the most beautiful woman I had ever seen. She was modest, cowering in her step. She was dressed in a green capulana, with a pattern of red cashews on it. She covered her face with the same capulana, as if shame were forcing her to conceal her identity. They both leaned against the wall. Ultímio spoke to her, but the girl

didn't respond. When Uncle began to walk away towards
the car, the girl shouted. It made my flesh creep, for it
wasn't the voice of a human being, but more like the cry
of a lowly animal. The words emerged covered in froth as
if her jaw were a law unto itself, divorced from the process
of thought.

—*Mali! Ni kumbela mali!*

She turned to me and, amid movements of the mouth
and spittle, was slow to produce those duplicated words.
Through gesture, I showed her that I didn't understand.
Ultímio shrugged his shoulders as he accelerated away. He
found it difficult to admit that he could no longer speak the
language of his birth.

—*The girl doesn't speak Portuguese, which is a pity.*

We returned home, the car skidding over the loose sand.
When he braked outside our front yard, a cloud of dust
was produced that seemed to please Ultímio. Such is the
poverty of our newly rich. They aren't rich. It's enough to
seem so. My uncle took his leave and made the following
announcement like some government edict: we would
proceed to bury the dead man, he had already arranged for
the ceremony, and paid for the services of a gravedigger.
Whether we wanted it or not.

—*But I am the master of ceremonies, Uncle.*

—*You'll be there, in your place, in your assigned place.*

12   *A visit to the maker of graves*

Do I have faith in God?
Yes, I suppose so.
But when it comes to belief, I believe in the Devil.
— *Grandpa Mariano*

Curozero Muando didn't see me arrive. I leaned against
the trunk of the mafurreira tree while I watched him. The
gravedigger was sitting next to a fire, his legs open and
almost brushing the flames. Over the flame, there was a
can of boiling water. Curozero was receiving the steam
on his face. Such is this type of heat that even the eyes
seem to be perspiring. That's how the gravediggers purify
themselves. They scratch around among the dust of the
dead, which is why they have to wash with water that hasn't
flowed across any soil.

The man was naked and didn't seem embarrassed by
my presence. After a while, he shivered as if feeling cold.
He got up and dried his head with a cloth, while he spoke
without looking at me.

—*Is it me you're looking for?*

—*Yes, is there another gravedigger round here?*

—*On the other side of the sky, there are gravediggers too.
Or rather the graveundiggers.*

He scorned my ignorance. What I didn't know was that
while the dead are buried here, over there, in the beyond,
they are unburied and celestified.

—*Yes, that's their job. And what's your job?*

—*My job?*

—*Yes, what have you come here for? Or would you ever
come and speak to me if you weren't in some difficulty?*

—*Well now, Curozero, I came here to...*

—*You don't need to provide an excuse. People don't
converse with gravediggers, that's how things are. My little
sister got so used to listening to silences that she never
developed the power of speech.*

But the profession, he said, had its science. The
gravedigger presented some of the most brilliant moments
of his career. And he explained what a complex piece of
engineering a grave could be. It's not easy opening up a
hole in the ground, the definitive hole. You have to lean
over like this, and he demonstrated: one leg back, the spine
bent and face at an angle, but never looking at the ground,
that never. The spade moving downwards without swiping
the air, oh no, for you didn't want to hit the ground and
injure the soil unnecessarily. It was the foot pressing the
top of the blade that cut the earth as if with love.

—*That's the art of it. It's the same as when you lay a sheet
of paper on your desk and begin to write on it.*

—*Well, Curozero, my friend, I've come here to ask
your opinion, you who deal with death. Do you think my
grandfather is really dead?*

—*In my current life, I don't have opinions. Only memories.*

And he remembered a lot, he remembered more than he had lived. Like those who keep little and take a lot. What he remembered best were the expressions of those who came to the cemetery to attend the burial of relatives and friends. Yes indeed, he remembered their fearful sadness, their vulnerable solitude. At that moment, everything becomes ephemeral, like a spider's web. Even their mixture of respect and fear was changing, as customs changed over time.

—*In the old days, they'd come and leave flowers here. Now they come to steal from the dead. They don't even respect the gods.*

—*What do you think has happened to my grandfather?*

It would be best if I never knew. For this was something that couldn't be explained in words. The gravedigger did his best to dissuade me:

—*You spent a lot of time away. Now you're a white man. Do you see what I'm saying? One finger doesn't catch a flea.*

—*What does that mean?*

—*You always need the other finger.*

You always need another finger, he repeated. And that finger is beyond both your hands. And what's more, he advised: I shouldn't look too hard. I should learn to leave mysteries in their due state. The wise man is the one who knows there are things he will never know. Things that are bigger than thought.

—*And besides, there's no problem: if the earth is hard, you can bury the man alive and kicking.*

—*But I don't want to bury Grandpa…*

—*Others do.*

Curozero gazed into infinity, shrugged his shoulders and clicked his tongue before speaking. At last, he was enlightening my understanding in the way I needed: that his death followed on from a life that had been lived badly. My Grandpa had committed a grave offence.

—*What offence?*

—*That's a secret he's carrying with him.*

To bury him like that, in this state of aborted death, would constitute a serious attack on Life itself. Instead of protecting us, the dead man would play havoc with the world. Even the rain would remain shut away, imprisoned in the clouds. And the earth would dry up, while the river would sink into the sand. He was insufficiently dead, a lightning flash that still remained to be blessed.

—*If you leave things to me, I know how to proceed.*

—*And how's that?*

—*This isn't an earthly but a watery matter. Your elders know that only too well. Ask them.*

It was then that I noticed the girl, the same one I had seen before with Uncle Ultímio. She was wearing the same green capulana, and had the same timid gestures. She advanced along the side of the wall, a bunch of flowers brushing against it. The petals were gradually falling off, fluttering wastefully to the ground.

—*This is Nyembeti, my sister. She's pretty, isn't she?*

Curozero directed the question at me and then stood watching me inquisitively. Something told me not to react. I gazed up at the sky distractedly. The gravedigger pressed on:

—*It's even painful, her beauty. Do you know what the problem is? It's that the girl can't speak straight, her tongue stumbles around her mouth, and her mouth stumbles around her head.*

—*Doesn't she say anything at all?* I asked, fearful.

—*No, she doesn't say anything at all.*

—*I don't understand, Curozero.*

—*My sister, Nyembeti, has never used any idea whatsoever.*

He began to get dressed while theorising about his sister. She used thought just as a crocodile swallows a stone. All it was good for was providing her existence with ballast, so that she could sink to the bottom effortlessly. When she needed air, she would regurgitate the stone, and now much lighter, she would float to the surface.

—*Be off with you!* he ordered Nyembeti. —*We want to talk alone.*

The girl leaned over me and offered me a flower. She shook it before giving it to me. Its petals fell to the ground in abundance.

—*Mali! Ni kumbela mali.*

The girl's spittle jumped as she tried to untangle her speech. I still remembered those words. They were precisely the ones she stuttered in her encounter with Ultímio.

—*What's she saying? Please translate for me.*

—*She's asking for money. It's the only thing she knows how to say.*

The gravedigger shrugged his shoulders with a half-amused smile, and concluded:

—*That's what she speaks now: the dialect of misery.*

His sister walked away. She rearranged her capulana as she went, now loosening it, now drawing it more closely about her. Her full body excited me. Was she completely naked underneath that piece of cloth. The gravedigger startled me in my interest.

—*Don't start dreaming about that girl. That's the advice of a friend!* Then, after a pause, he continued: —*And now I want to ask you something.*

—*Ask away, Curozero.*

—*You can see that I'm the only gravedigger round here. Now, let me ask you: when I die, who is going to bury me?*

I swallowed an entire desert, having guessed his request. Curozero was charging me with the responsibility of burying him. And he seemed to be talking seriously, as if claiming that I had already made him that promise.

—*Will you do it for me, sir?*

—*Me?*

He burst out laughing and patted me on the back. I should relax, he was just testing me.

—*I don't need to be buried.*

I looked to see if I could glimpse the beautiful girl. There she was. She must have known I was looking for she let her capulana slip off. With my heart thumping, I was able to confirm that she had nothing on underneath. Curozero interrupted my vision.

—*And now, taking advantage of your visit, come with me: I want to show you some work of mine, my best work yet.*

He led me to the end of his plot of land, right next to the rear wall. He pointed to a grave. That was where Juca

Sabão had been laid to rest. Curozero had dug the grave
for his own father, old Sabão. He didn't weep, for it was
the finest grave he had ever dug. The whole Island was
watching him. He had to show them that grave digging
was a skilled and honourable profession. This type of
task wasn't just for anyone. So not a tear was shed or a
sigh uttered. The funeral ended, everyone withdrew, and
the cemetery was left empty. That night, it rained, and he
knew that it wasn't just rain. He left his house, went to the
cemetery and sat down next to the grave. While the rain
ran down his body, he wept, he wept and wept. He wept
ceaselessly for as long as it rained. Until it didn't hurt any
more. He had been washed, the heavens had assuaged his
yearning and his silence.

Juca Sabão shot just like that, an innocent life gunned
down at point-blank range, was something that had never
been witnessed before in Luar-do-Chão. But revenge
would come. A bullet has two ends. Its victim is killed by
one of them. And the killer invariably succumbs to the
other. The gravedigger had learned many a thing. Death is
dark: who said that? Well, he himself, Curozero Muando,
had once been on the edge of death, on his opposite side.
While he was asleep, he had been attacked by a hyena, and
had escaped by the skin of his teeth. He had summoned
his entire family and explained: death, he could indeed
confirm, was an intense flash of light, a star exploding.
It was like a sun coming into one's range of vision to the
point where everything was visible, even in shadow. He
said it now and said it again: thick shadow, and the future
turned suddenly into past.

—*We don't go to heaven. It's the other way round: heaven enters us through our lungs. A dying person chokes on a cloud.*

I looked again to see whether I could still catch a glimpse of the beautiful Nyembeti. But no. The only thing left was the capulana laid out to dry, moving in gently sensual undulation. Clothes receive the soul of those who wear them.

13   *Some very white powders*

A man drowns where the water is calmest.
—*African proverb*

—*He's in the refrigerator! That's where you'll find him.*

At the fish-processing plant everyone was talking at the top of their voices. The noise of the generator stifled speech and they had to yell in order to tell me where my father was. I didn't need it confirmed. For at that very instant, my old man stepped out of the cold store, as frigid as a piece of hake. What was he doing? He was visiting the refrigerators to see if he could find accommodation for Grandpa Mariano.

—*But Father, I agree with Grandma Dulcineusa. How can we keep Grandpa here, along with all the sea trout?*

My father laughed. After all, wasn't that where he'd always been, with trout, except that they had two legs, mermaids with human lower halves? And he guffawed. I shouldn't take him seriously, he'd just come to visit a friend who was working there. Or did I doubt his moral rectitude? But what he wanted was to avoid serious matters. He felt like some light-hearted conversation, he wanted to pollute his chest with a cigarette or two, to cast his eyes over a few girls.

—*They haven't managed to drive me completely crazy yet. Come to Tuzébio's bar with me. I need to wet my whistle.*

On the way, I told him about my meeting with Ultímio. My father reacted angrily. He shouted:

—*Ultímio's a scumbag!*

—*Don't talk like that, Father. Ultímio's an uncle, we've got to unite the family at a time like this...*

—*That's for the fairies. We call that type of talk a wasp's spittle round here.*

I wanted to keep the stone moist, but there wasn't enough water. I shouldn't waste my time. Ultímio didn't deserve it. For that uncle of mine, along with his wife and children, were driven by haste and by greed. They wanted it all and quickly. They were like the colonials of old: one look at the land and they were already thinking: I wish that was mine. But as far as we knew, the land had no proprietor. There was no living owner. The only proprietors worthy of trust are the dead, those who live there. Like Grandpa, who was getting ready to take possession of the ground.

—*A scumbag! That uncle of yours is nothing more than a scumbag!*

My father repeated these grim curses that no brother is worthy of. It was his rage that left me mystified. They were hiding something from me.

—*What's happening here, Father?*

—*Nothing's happening. Nothing has ever happened in Luar-do-Chão.*

—*I'm not talking about the Island. I'm talking about Uncle Ultímio, and all this hatred that must have some explanation. Don't hide anything from me, Father. I need to know.*

—*What's happening, my son, is drugs. That's what's happening.*

—*Drugs?*

—*They're looking for drugs, a consignment of drugs that was landed here and disappeared.*

That was only what he suspected. But he had made sense of it all. That some traffickers from the city thought old Mariano knew the whereabouts of the consignment. Grandpa was pretending to be dead so as not to have to confess.

—*They suspect I know something, because I used to give my father a hand.*

—*Did Grandpa never mention anything?*

—*Never. Now he's in that state, neither here nor there, but he never admitted to me where he had buried the wretched cargo.*

Who knows, maybe Grandpa was like this, between frontiers, in order to save us? My old man even asked himself: that sacrifice of his, feigning death, might it not be a generous act in order to protect us from the big-time villains?

To keep our order of priorities, we first needed to have our patriarch's death confirmed. That's why Doctor Mascarenha had been summoned. Even though he'd virtually ceased his doctorly duties, the Goan was above suspicion. He couldn't be bought.

—*Uncle Ultímio says he's going to call another doctor. To sign the death certificate.*

—*Do you know what we ought to do? What we should do is go ahead and have Grandpa buried.*

—*What? We can't, Father. Don't you see that...*

—*Wait a moment. It's something that's just occurred to me. A pretend burial, just to deceive the crooks.*

—*But Father, there are some things one can't just pretend to do. A pretend burial?*

He told me to keep quiet. We had reached Tuzébio's bar. Before stepping through the door my old man asked me to keep a secret. Everything he had said was to remain with me. I placed my finger on my lips as a sign that I agreed to the promise.

People crowded round to greet us. And they invited us to join in their celebration. No one knew exactly what was being celebrated. But drinks were passed round rapidly, and merriment fed yet more merriment. The doctor raised his glass and suggested a toast.

—*Who are you going to toast, Mascarenha? Yes, whose health does a doctor drink to?*

—*I drink to my own health. Me, Amílcar Mascarenha.*

—*To yourself?*

—*It's because I'm leaving the Island tomorrow.*

—*You're leaving? Why?*

—*I received orders to leave.*

—*Orders from whom?*

Mascarenha didn't want to comment further on the matter. But he was decisive with regard to the direction his life was going to take. Those around him commented:

—*The man's afraid.*

—*That wasn't an order. What he received were threats.*

—*And he's right to feel scared. Those people kill.*

Silence fell. There was no one left to talk to. I went back to the house. I should have gone to sleep off the heat of the day. But I decided to write. I went to the garden, and sat down in the shade of the mango tree. I took my notepad. I jotted down ideas, loose sentences. It was at that point that the unbelievable happened: my handwriting began to disobey the hand that engendered it. What I was writing was transformed into something else. Another letter emerged from my hand, without me being able to stop myself:

Do you want to know about the white powder, the stuff that brought blood and mourning to this place? You, my dear grandson, are casting the bait further than the hook. Be in no doubt, child: you didn't come here summoned for the funeral of a live person. You were called here by the death of this whole place. Luar-do-Chão began to die the day they murdered my friend, Juca Sabão. Didn't his son, the gravedigger, tell you the whole story? Well, I'm going to tell you what happened.

They pumped a couple of bullets into my friend because of some bags they had brought from the city and left in the store room. Juca didn't know anything about it. Except that there were a couple of bags, the contents of which he was unaware, under an old piece of canvas. The person who'd brought

*them was that Josseldo, Juca's nephew. He would
turn up with some pretty undesirable company, some
mischief-makers with shaven heads, a bunch capable
of taking your breath away. And there were others
who were even more colourful, with kerchiefs tied
round their heads. Even Dulcineusa was surprised:
macho men with kerchiefs, were they pretending to
be women? And shaved heads when there was no
mourning to explain it? Dear God, how times have
changed. I've said it before and I'll say it again:
Jesus bled and Mary wept.*

*Well anyway, Juca Sabão didn't like what he saw.
They couldn't be up to any good. So he came to talk
to me about his anxieties. At first, he'd thought of
burying the bags down by the marshes. Did I think
that would be the right place? But I wanted time to
think. What had the ruffians told him?*

—Yes, what did they say?

*They said that those bags would bring prosperity
to Luar-do-Chão. And so I supported Juca in his
thoughts. He should reflect on the matter: if it was
something that was going to bring prosperity to the
place, what could it be? Yes, indeed, what could it be
unless it were fertiliser, manures of the type that they
made in the cities?*

*Think carefully, Juca, my friend. It's fertiliser, all
full of compounds and chemicals.*

*He meditated, adding further ideas to his
argument. Finally, he agreed. And so, convinced
that that was what they contained, Juca Sabão*

*and I spread the powder over the arable land. We
emptied bags and bags across the countryside, mixing
everything with the sand so that the soil should be
given its sustenance. All we'd have to do was wait
for the rains to come and we'd be able to watch the
green appearing, like mould on yesterday's bread.*

*But then, Josseldo and his selfsame friends
from the city arrived and began to ask after their
merchandise. Where were the bags? It was a tense
conversation, full of threats of knives and blood.
Until those in charge made Juca take them to where
the bags had been emptied. But my friend had
forgotten. There was no ill intention, it was all true,
a genuine loss of memory. My pal Juca asked:*

*—In what place? But everywhere is a place.
That's where I spread the fertiliser, out there and
all over.*

*It must have dissolved among the roots, merged
with the sands. To illustrate the point, Juca Sabão
bent down and picked up a handful of soil.*

—It's all here, among this endless stretch of earth.

*The strangers didn't believe him. They screamed,
threatened, and then resorted to physical argument.
They tried to extract a confession from him with
kicks and blows. Did his nephew try and defend
his uncle? No, the boy was the most violent of them
all. They all but beat the life out of my friend. Until
one of them, gun in hand, aimed at Juca Sabão's big
old head. There was a shot, and then it was just a
question of watching how blood flows out of the body*

*like a snake slithering along. But he never dropped
the soil he held in his hand. He was the one who fell
to the ground, hard and heavy. But the soil cupped
in his hands, that remained for ever cradled in Juca's
dying gesture.*

*On the day of poor Juca's funeral, I was assailed
by one certainty: you must save Luar-do-Chão. Yes,
what we needed was someone from outside, but
who was also an insider. I came to this conclusion
as I thought how the breath of life and the flurry of
death mingled in our Island. In burying Juca, we
were laying undeserved bones in the earth's belly. The
ground would punish us all for it in due course.*

*Do you know what I feel when I remember my
buddy Juca Sabão? I envy him, I envy him so much,
dear God. How shameful, don't you see? Envy is a
mean little sentiment that we devote to people over
mundane things. I envy Sabão not for anything he
possessed, but for the way he died. My friend took
with him his own piece of earth. Do you understand
me? Juca didn't wait for others to cast their clods
over him. It was he who threw the first handful of
sand over himself.*

14 *The earth closed*

The moon travels slowly,
but it crosses the world.
— *African proverb*

At long last, Grandpa's funeral. Incomplete, but still
happening, solemn and inevitable. With neither a dead man
nor a body, but with pomp and ceremony. They decided
to have the burial to keep some people happy. Some of the
family were getting impatient. Some wanted to go home and
needed to take their leave of the eldest of the Malilanes. They
needed to say farewell, even if it was only half a one.

The whole Island filled the cemetery. The women
mourners were at the entrance, sowing tearful chants,
while relatives filed in from both sides of the gate. The
gravedigger was awaited to begin the final part of the ritual.

But the coffin was still at home. And there, in the
roofless room, Mariano's body still lay outside the coffin,
waiting for whatever might be. Grandpa waited in the
exclusive company of his spouse, Dulcineusa. Only after
the grave had been dug and the first blessings uttered, only
then would the tractor come and fetch Dito Mariano.

At last, Curozero Muando made his entrance, dragging his spade behind him. In spite of his apparent casualness, there was a certain dignity about him: he was, after all, the only gravedigger in Luar-do-Chão. He pushed his way through the solemn crowd, chortling a song:

—*I swear, I give you my word, this is truly how I'll die.*

He stubbed out his cigarette on the handle of his spade, spat in his hands in preparation for his arduous task.

Abstinêncio suggested to my father:

—*Go and ask him not to sing that song.*

The gravedigger raised his spade with a doleful gesture. The metal glimmered and flashed in the air, before descending like an arrow to the ground. But instead of a soft thud, a loud clank was heard, the scraping of metal against metal. The spade glittered, skidded like a horse's hoof and slipped speedily out of his hand. I could scarcely contain my astonishment: were those sparks flying? Or was it the ndlati bird that had swooped down on to our earthly sod? What was certain was that the spade had hit something hard, so hard that its blade was twisted. Curozero Muando looked at the instrument, and looked again, shook his head and then gazed at those assembled as if awaiting instructions. My uncles, however, remained silent, in a heightened state of nerves. A cloud hung heavily over the place.

The gravedigger decided to try and dig a grave further to one side. A murmur went through those present. Curozero, sweating profusely, took a few steps and began his battle with the ground once again. In vain. Even there, there was an insurmountable piece of rock at the surface

of the ground. Someone issued an order: he should try
to dig a third grave well away from there. Once again,
the spade scraped against a hard surface. Uncle Ultímio
stepped forward decisively, and grabbed the spade from the
gravedigger's hands.

—*Give me that shovel!*

With an air of determination, he hurled the spade
against the ground. Once again it hit some obscure chunk
of rock. A shiver went through everyone's spirit. They
called the gravedigger aside and asked him:

—*What's happening?*

—*I don't know, bosses, I've never seen anything like it. It's
as if the earth had closed itself.*

—*How has it closed itself?*

—*I don't know. I'm all confused.*

—*Get digging. Dig over there, by that tree.*

The gravedigger went over to the frangipani tree, in
a corner of the cemetery. But once again, he came up
against the ground. There was the same clash of metals
announcing some impenetrable substratum. Despair
increased.

Suddenly my father, by now unhinged, began to shout:
he shouldn't be digging with a metal instrument. It injured
the soil. Having said this, he knelt down and began to
dig with his hands. He dug desperately, salivating with
the effort. In a short time, his fingers were all bloody. My
father's despair showed in his very flesh, and he moaned
and swore. As the earth piled up, it was red with blood.
Until Abstinêncio prodded him with his foot, signalling
him to stop. Uncle issued his command:

—*Stop this, you're just making things worse!*

Dripping like this, without flowing through the proper channels, blood is a poison that infects the deceased and the whole family as well. People were getting nervous, my uncles were beginning to argue among themselves:

—*This is witchcraft, brother. This is the result of a spell.*

—*A spell against whom? Certainly not against me.*

—*Well, who is it against, then?*

—*Against us, for fuck's sake! Against us. Against us.*

—*What do you mean, against us? You speak for yourself, Abstinêncio.*

—*It was your fault, Ultímio, you betrayed the laws of tradition.*

—*What laws, for fuck's sake?*

—*You got the government over there to line your pockets. You forgot your family, Ultímio.*

The argument stopped as the gravedigger approached, his shoulders drooping.

—*So did you have any luck?*

He gave a mournful shake of his head. His mouth suffered from lapses of memory: he invariably forgot to close it. He had looked around in the vicinity, searching for a piece of diggable terrain that might do for a grave. But the result was always the same. Curozero suggested we go home, while he continued to try and solve the problem. He would go over the whole terrain with his spade at the ready.

—*Tomorrow, you gentlemen will come back and find a nicely dug little grave.*

His voice was too shaky for someone making a promise.

With a vague wave of the arm, he summoned us near. And suggested:

—*At the same time, you should organise a watch. The dead get stolen round here.*

—*We'll pay a policeman,* said Uncle Ultímio. —*I'll pay, you can leave it to me.*

—*That's not enough, my friends,* the gravedigger replied. —*You don't know this neighbourhood, sir. Round here, you need to concrete over the ground. Otherwise, they dig down into the soil looking for coffins.*

—*We haven't even got a grave yet, and we're already thinking of defending it?*

We were interrupted by the unexpected arrival of Nyembeti. The gravedigger's sister stood, submissive, wrapped in silence and respect. Only later did she pass a wad of notes to Ultímio. No one except for Curozero could hear what she said. It was he who, embarrassed, translated what his sister said:

—*Teka mali yako. That's what she's saying. She's giving you back your money.*

Uncle Ultímio was as surprised as he was irritated. He hunched his shoulders, and his tone of voice turned militaristic. He pointed at Curozero Muando and issued his command:

—*I want all this resolved by tomorrow.*

—*I don't take orders from you, sir, or from anyone else.*

Everyone looked at each other, astonished. Had the gravedigger suddenly jettisoned his servile countenance? Looking at Curozero Muando, no one was left in any doubt. The man spoke as if his tongue were as pointed as his shoes. He had worked for others all his life. Or at least, that was only the appearance. For in reality, he had worked for life itself.

—*My only boss is life.*

Ultímio still muttered some threats before turning his back. My other uncles withdrew, while the girl too walked off. I was the only one left to keep Curozero Muando company. Keeping him company is just a figure of speech, for in fact the gravedigger didn't pause. He was busy, like a wild bore snuffling at the ground. Later, he stopped and sat on the wall. I went over to him, but didn't speak. It was a way of showing him respect. And I waited for him to say something, without hurrying him. Finally, he spoke:

—*I'm going to tell you something now that we're alone. As far as I'm concerned, this is vengeance.*

—*Whose vengeance?*

The gravedigger looked around to make sure there was no one else present, and explained: it was the earth's vengeance against the waywardness of the living. I should think about the amount of rubbish they were burying all over the place, dirtying the earth's depths and polluting sources. Word was going round that even drugs had been mixed with the sand out in the country. What was happening in that cemetery was the earth protesting against mankind.

—*The earth protesting?* I asked.

—*Didn't you know? The earth dies just like a person.*

What was happening therefore had a perfectly simple explanation: the earth had perished. Just as a body may be reduced to a skeleton, the earth had been reduced to its bare bones. It no longer had a shoulder, only a shoulder blade. It was devoid of grain or dust. Just a thick amalgam, a cold stone.

—*But there's no logic in that.*

—*Everything here has its logic, my friend. I've already told you: you're going around catching fleas with one finger.*

The war was to blame for a lot, the gravedigger continued. They buried a lot of people who'd been shot, and the lead had leaked out of their bodies into the ground. Now, there were no longer graves, nor bottom to the earth. We couldn't even extract soil from the soil. It's the earth's vengeance, he repeated.

Over in the distance, the figure of Nyembeti passed by, dressed in black over her dark skin. A cloud of mosquitoes sent me their warning: it was time to go. But Curozero Muando still wanted to say something. He spoke in a low tone, behind the hand that he held up to his mouth.

—*A little while ago I was rude to your uncle. I don't know what came over me...*

—*It's natural, you're nervous, Curozero.*

—*It's the disgusting things he's doing with Nyembeti. I ask you: can money buy a life?*

—*Calm down, Curozero. Forget Uncle Ultímio.*

—*It's just that you can bury a dead man. But you can never bury your fear.*

—*You shouldn't be afraid, brother.*

—*You've forgotten. Round here, fear is the first thing you learn to have.*

—*But do you have any reason to be afraid?*

—*Can't you see. Are you more blind than a mole? Or do you only have eyes to peer at another man's sister?*

—*Peer at your sister. But I've never looked...*

—*I'm sorry. I was just talking for the sake of it. It's my nerves that are letting me say inappropriate things.*

We should leave these considerations behind. The problem now was this impossible burial. I should go home and have a good think. For the confusion was not just about the earth's refusal to open. It was the dead man who refused to be put away in it. That was the other reason for his fear. I tried to pour water on the flame:

—*Now, don't take things so seriously, Curozero. You know what Grandpa Mariano is like!*

For Dito Mariano, with his immense laziness, dying must be hard work. It just happened that he was a long time in taking the final step.

—*In life, did he ever appear when we expected? Well then, now that our expectations are being dashed, he is refusing to disappear.*

When I got home, my soul was buffeted by unease. I was pursued by the image of my father digging in despair. I even dreamed about it at night. Over a huge expanse of bare, red ground, I could see dozens of holes that he had made. My old man, Fulano Malta, raised his head and declared:

—*I'm not opening up graves for the dead man, your respected grandfather. I'm burying myself alive, while I've still got the strength.*

15 The dream

I'm more and more like a crab:
my eyes are outside my body,
I dream sideways,
undecided between two souls:
one belonging to water and the other to dry land.
— *Curozero Muando*

Here's what I dreamed: that the gravedigger, Curozero Muando, had dug the soil outside the cemetery, far from the town. He had sought out the most remote spots, on the edge of lagoons, in the foothills of the Zipene, in the valleys of Xitulundo. Everywhere, it was the same: it was impossible to penetrate the soil. He'd even tried in the secret shadows of Xinhambanine, the sacred forest of the elders. The gravedigger had fallen to his knees amid the sand: let the gods help us and soften the earth. But neither prayer nor lamentation had any effect. The spade inevitably hit a hard sheet of stone. It was as if the earth had closed up everywhere.

Friends arrived from the city and told me that the same

thing was happening elsewhere. Throughout the country, the earth was refusing to open its belly to human design. I sent messages abroad. And the same was happening there. In every continent, the ground had grown hard, impenetrable. The problem had become catastrophic and global in proportion. It wasn't just a question of not being able to bury the dead. Agriculture had become paralysed. Construction projects, mines, dredging the ports, everything was at a standstill.

International leaders sought speedy explanations, scientists of considerable repute carried out research into possible reasons, commissions proliferated, there were journeys and expeditions. No one had any idea that the root of all this disequilibrium could be found, after all, right here in our Island. No one realised that everything had begun in the person of Grandpa Mariano.

In my dream, I went back to the cemetery. I couldn't find the gravedigger, Curozero. But his sister, Nyembeti, was there, more inviting than ever, dressed in her swift-moving capulana that revealed more than it concealed.

Inviting me with gestures and whistles, the girl led me to a place that only she knew of, at the bottom of a hill. She chose her path amid rocks and caves and then entered a hidden refuge. There where the light scarcely penetrated, she lay down on the dark earth and called me. It was a gloomy cavern and the smell was familiar to me. I hesitated before lying down on the ground. It frightened me that I couldn't see where I was.

—*Lie on top of me!*

Was Nyembeti speaking? And was she speaking

in Portuguese? I covered her with my body, my arms
supporting me so that I shouldn't be too heavy on her.
But she pulled at my wrists and led my hands to cover her
breasts. And then to visit her body and her moist secrets.
There in the darkness, we made love. Our groans grew
loud, echoing through the roundness of the cave. Finally,
a bird took to the wing from the ceiling, lightening the
gloom with its whiteness.

I only noticed when, breathless, I began to regain my
composure: the smell in that cave was the same as in the
lumber room. And the taste of that woman, her voice,
her scent, everything about her was the same. Could
Nyembeti have been at Nyumba-Kaya on that day? Could
she have been the unknown lover who had assailed me
once before?

—*Are you surprised that I speak Portuguese?*

I was astonished to hear her speak. But the girl
explained: she wanted to escape from the various Ultímios
who had presented themselves to her, with their city
ways. That's why she behaved as she did, idiotically and
indigenously, to shield herself from their intentions.

—*With you, I can speak any language. And even in no
language at all.*

We kissed. Once again, I had the sensation of returning
to the lumber room. Her arm pushed me away, gently but
without hesitation.

—*Now, come with me. I brought you here to show you
something.*

With her hands cupped, she dug into the earth. And
I was dumbstruck. The soil there was soft, flaky, apt for

burrowing. Nyembeti had discovered a place for Grandpa's tomb to be dug.

—*How did you find this place?*

But she wouldn't accept my question. Places aren't found, they're built. The difference in that piece of ground was not geographical. She pointed to both of us, entwined our hands, and then placed them on her heart. Did she mean that the earth had become like that because we had made love on it? Could the earth be regained through love? Could it be that by making the ground our marriage bed, we were softening it, reconciling ourselves with our most ancient of dwelling places? Maybe. Perhaps everything was as simple as old Mariano's sheet, the one he was now resting on. Who knows whether it wasn't that old sheet, with all its smells of past loves, that selfsame sheet that was holding the old man back in life.

Nyembeti looked at me, curious at my absent gaze. She smiled and with a gesture suggested that I should return to town. She would remain in the cave. She even made me a request as she said goodbye:

—*I know that you'll go back to the city. But when you return, bring me a present by way of a memento.*

It was strange what she asked me to bring her: snake's saliva, lizard's spittle. Or if I could, even better: the sap of poisonous trees, cactus slime. Anything as long as it belonged to the category of venom, the mortal mixtures that certain animals concoct in the most infernal parts of their insides. That's what I dreamed on that hot night.

Early in the morning, I got up and wandered off. I needed to recover from the visions I'd had in my previous dream. All I wanted was to visit the past. I made for the slopes where, as a child, I had driven the family flocks to pasture. The goats were still there, in a variety of dappled tones. They looked the same as they always had, as if they'd forgotten to die. They wandered away unhurriedly, to let me by. As far as they were concerned, any man who came along must be a shepherd. And they had a point. I don't know anyone in Luar-do-Chão who hasn't tended goats.

I owe my ability to dream to being a shepherd. It was a shepherd who invented the first dream. Out there, faced with nothingness, merely waiting for time, any shepherd would weave fantasies with the thread of his solitude.

The goats cast me into memories of olden times. And the face of my sweet mother, Mariavilhosa, misted my eyes. For out in those pastures, her face had often visited me, seeking refuge in my little soul. My mother had become pregnant previous to me. But something had gone wrong. It was said that she had had a miscarriage, but the story had become distorted over time. The doctor, ever the same Mascarenha, had told Dona Mariavilhosa that she would never conceive again. But medicine had been wrong, and there I was as proof. After me, my mother had become pregnant again. But the old prophecy was confirmed on that occasion. My little brother, inside her womb, had been unable to embrace life. For Mariavilhosa, that was reason enough to go mad. It might seem strange, but the delivery – if we can call such an empty act a delivery – occurred on the night the country became independent. On that very night, as the town was celebrating the unleashing of an entire future, my mother was dying of a past: the cold body of the child who would have been her third son. My father took me inside while Mariavilhosa, carrying the newly dead baby in her arms, dragged herself across the yard. We even saw her raise the baby's body to show it to the new moon. Just as one does with the newly born. My father gave her a piece of burning wood. And she hurled the cindered stick up at the moon while shouting:

—*Take it, moon, take your husband!*

That piece of fire tearing through the darkness became etched on my memory as if it were a star rising high into the sky before falling in a thousand cadences of light. Years later, when my mother was already dead, I looked up at the moon while tending my flock at night, and saw Mariavilhosa with her child on her back. And I heard her cry of affliction, stung by the barb of hunger. So I ran to the fire I had lit and doused the flames. By killing the fire, I was exposing myself to wild animals and the cold. But that wasn't important. Only in the darkness could my mother find comfort and sustenance. It was in that spot that she was able to quieten my dead brother, the child who, because it had never lived, would never die.

16 *The ideas of an animal*

See what life is like: I have two
hearts, and only led half a life.
I was born on the day when two suns shone in
the sky. And yet for me, it was always night.
— *Grandpa Mariano*

*Can the earth soften by force of love? Only if love
is rain that moistens our soul from inside. But you
shouldn't put words to such thoughts. For that is the
idea of an animal, my son. Only an animal knows
that there is no difference or variety in rain. Rain
is all one. It's always the same rain, just interrupted
from time to time. So the earth being closed is
a matter that escapes you, animals, and living
creatures. For its occurrence has no cause. It just has
a reason to happen.*
  *This land began to die the moment we began to
want to be others, from another existence, another
place. Luar-do-Chão died when those who ruled
it stopped loving it. But the earth doesn't die any
more than the river stops flowing. Let things be, the*

ground will open again when I enter my death in all serenity. That's why you must listen to me. Listen to me, my son.

I always had the thoughts of a dullard, dry in my judgements. For I, Mariano, my dear Grandson, I was still very young when I began to grow old. Just like now: I began to die when I was still alive. To die gradually, unawares, was never something I found difficult. But to become old, yes, I certainly did. Becoming ever more sluggish didn't just make me sad. Worse, it made me ashamed. This decline made me bend under a weight that came from inside me, as if I were becoming pregnant with my own death and felt the growing presence, inside me, of that foetus that was my own end. I even thought of my own daughter-in-law's sadness, your late mother, who knew the baby she was carrying was dead in her womb. And yet she stroked her belly, while looking up at the full moon, just as one does to bring good fortune to the soon to be born. Your mother, Dona Mariavilhosa, was a woman of courage and dignity. She died in the river, which is a way of not dying. She wished she had had many children. But you, in the end, were the only one. All time is in your hands, like a sea with only one wave. You should go and visit her grave. You should take a few handfuls of the soil that covers her and spread it around the fields to see if the place can be purified.

See? We always end up talking about them, those much maligned women. In the beginning, they *were beyond my powers of reasoning. But as I grew older I became more able to understand women. If I found it difficult to love them, I gained another type of affection for those creatures. The less I needed my body to jump on top of their attractions, the more I began to identify with them, almost to find in myself similarities with them.*

Until I reached that stage when age turns into an illness. There were times when I thought of suicide. But then I'd pour myself a little glass of something and in no more than a few seconds, my self-belief was restored. But then I'd have a relapse. If only God would carry me off, just as he had João Felizbento, the crazy newspaper man, who collected old papers from the quarter where the whites lived. He was carried off by God as if he were by now an old newspaper. I would have liked that to happen to me, turned into something that no longer had any use, it being enough for God to bend down and pick up that useless utensil.

Sometimes, I put my faith in illness: some incurable infirmity that would carry me off. On some occasions, my wish was nearly fulfilled: I would wake up all swollen and give thanks, in the hope that my inner waters would grow like a September tide. And I would spend the day watching my middle finger, swollen like a conger. My slippers would disappear, jammed in between puffed-up flesh. At that time, I didn't use shoelaces. I would go out into the street, just wearing my slippers.

Barefoot certainly not. A black man doesn't walk barefoot unless he's being punished, condemned to relive his past. Poverty is about walking next to the ground, not fearful of treading on something, but of being trodden on. For the poisonous thorn doesn't spike a person's foot, but his heart.

So in the end, what was left of my soul? An accumulation of things yearned for. My soul is a piece of old iron in the mechanic João Celestioso's scrapyard. Yearning is like rust: you scratch it away expecting to clean it, only to find you're sowing more rust. That was what now made me suffer most. Yearning for a nice glass of something, a yearning for having a healthy body and not being aware of it, even a yearning for the time I could pee good and hard. A yearning for the tastes of life, of those flavours that awaited me. Not a meal to eat, no, but life itself served up on plates that always gleamed.

Let me tell you this, my dear Grandson: although my flame has been extinguished, I still have a glimmer of life in me, the shadow of a robust spirit. So much so that at the moment when I was stricken with this death, a spell was cast over the whole town. My eyes were losing their lustre, my chest was fading, but at that precise moment, fires were flickering in every house as if a sudden, imperceptible breeze were blowing up. And then, they died down, blown out by this thick shadow. They were extinguished at the exact moment the cameras flashed that were taking my photograph.

You asked the reasons for my extinction.
Well, that's how it happened. And don't occupy
or preoccupy yourself over it. For you, my dear
Grandson, are carrying out your duties well.
Supporting your grandmother, calming your uncles,
dampening fears and apparitions. What you had to
do for your family is almost done. Almost. But the
most painful part is yet to come.

17 *In prison*

For some, life buries more than
death. For I only lived in two states:
inearthed and unearthed.
— *Grandpa Mariano*

In the mulatto Tuzébio's bar, there was a general atmosphere
of excitement. Everyone was talking loudly, their gestures
and voices hovering over their glasses of beer. Their speech
was like the foam, whipped up by obstinacy. There was only
one topic of conversation: the curse that had befallen the
land. They'd seen every type of disaster: plagues of locusts,
droughts that crack stones, fires that had swallowed up
granaries, floods that had lapped against whole landscapes.
But the ground closing up, this was something no one
had ever seen before. The sands turning to stone were a
punishment of the sort no one could remember.

And where to find a reason for such punishment?
Whose fault was it? People were scared to even speculate
on the causes of such a disaster. Truth is like a nest of
vipers. You recognise it not by seeing it, but by the gravity
of its bite. Some people advised me:

—*The best thing you can do is leave the Island. You're a marked man.*

To be marked is to be the bearer of disaster. No single person is only one life. No place is only one place. In this place, spirits dwell everywhere, revealing hidden beings. And I had awoken ancient ghosts.

—*They're going to say it was you, Mariano.*

—*Me, why?*

—*It stopped raining when you arrived, the earth closed up after you came here. It's all coincidence, my dear friend. And we all know that coincidences happen, but never exist.*

My father rowed against the general current, making his powerful voice heard above all the others:

—*Don't leave here, son. In fact, you never did leave Luar-do-Chão in the first place.*

I feigned consent, listened to orders and advice without replying, saying yes or even maybe. I was learning the habits of the place, listening while appearing to be phlegmatic. What is it that is so far away that everybody catches a better glimpse of it inside us? The horizon. Well, I was beyond the horizon. A certainty had established itself within me: my obligation was to my grandfather, Mariano, and I had to fulfil his recommendations.

I left the bar, as if in a daze. In reality, I hadn't drunk more than half a glass, enough to warm up my forgetfulness. I paused along the darkened road. I urinated next to a tree trunk, liberating my recent intake. I heard the wind high above threading its way through the leaves of the coconut trees. Along the side of the track, some children, up late, were cracking open coconuts. Young

girls braided hair. When I was a child, it would have been
impossible to find kids outside at that hour. Did these
children have no one to summon them home? Maybe it all
confirmed what Grandpa had said: all these children are
orphans, even those with both parents alive. They will for
ever be like young birds: they will never yearn for the nest.

Suddenly, I noticed two policemen coming towards me
along the same path. They were doing a routine search of
the shops for sure. But as they passed me, they held me and
immediately started tying my arms. Astonished, I barely
reacted. Subdued by such violent treatment, I was led back
to the police station. The administrator sat waiting for
me, with studied self-importance. He had a peevish look
about him, and without beating about the bush, he fired a
question at me with heavy voice:

—*Did you urinate on the ground?*

I didn't understand immediately. But there was a
hidden suspicion. I was the cause of all this terrestrial
disorder. Being a warm-blooded man, my urine might
be hot enough to melt any subterranean minerals. The
administrator pressed on, sensing he was on to something:

—*Have you had sex these last few days?*

Anger locked my voice in my throat. My rancour was
increasing, and I was already losing control of myself when
I fired another question back:

—*Do my uncles know I'm here?*

I realised too late that I shouldn't have asked. For the
question caused the administrator to get on his high horse
in order to show me who was boss. In the pursuit of his
idea, the man became irritated: cemeteries are for those

who are dead, life is for those who are alive. The worm has been burrowing holes without permission, he said. And he went on with his interrogation:

—*What were you doing in the cemetery, what were you and the gravedigger talking about?*

Tension was growing. The policemen didn't point their pistols at me, but their eyes were like vultures as they looked at me. What would Grandpa have done in those circumstances? And I thought to myself: how curious it was that I was looking to the old man for inspiration. I was, after all, learning to behave like a Malilane. And then suddenly, I received the answer in a flash: Mariano would pretend he was dead. So that's what I decided to do. And it proved to be the best course of action at that moment. For what was being talked about in that police station was not what people were saying. It wasn't the earth closing up that they were interested in. They were suspicious of something else: that I was meddling around in the murder of Juca Sabão. With my city slicker's smartness, I was stirring up what was already dead and buried. I was the so-called inquisitive worm.

As I wouldn't answer, they took off my shoes and ordered me to sit on the ground. And there I stayed, only then becoming aware of how much the ropes were digging into my wrists.

In the meantime, news of my arrest had reached Tuzébio's bar. My father shot off and, without more ado, burst into the police station, remonstrating loudly. The administrator clarified the situation impassively:

—*Your son hasn't been arrested, he's just detained.*

—*Well, in that case, I haven't come to free him, just to let him go*, Fulano replied.

And as if handling a child, he seized me by the collar and dragged me off across the room. One of the policemen blocked his way and pushed my father up against a wall. There was a kick, and then another one. My father bent double in a corner of the room, while coming to terms with each pain in turn.

—*Stop this immediately!*

It was my Uncle Ultímio issuing the order. Without my noticing, he had come in through one of the inner doors of the police station, one of the ones that gave direct access from the administrative building. The policemen stood back. My father stood up straight.

—*Come on, son. Let's go.*

I still expected the authorities to come after us. But no. We left the police station and walked through the crowd that had accumulated round the building. Fulano Malta wasn't for exchanging conversation, but even so, he led me along with my hands still tied behind my back. We went to the quay. There we remained, the two of us, surrounded by darkness. He gazed at the waters. As if his eyes were oars and were dipping into the river against the current. A good man wears his heart on his shoe, at the mercy of those who would tread on it. After a long silence, he muttered:

—*I'm sorry.*

—*Father, you're saying sorry to me?*

—*Not to you. To Juca Sabão. It's him I'm asking for forgiveness.*

—*Aren't you going to untie me, Father?*

He smiled, a rictus that was the product of sadness. He had been distracted, alert to his own ghosts. He undid the ropes and looked closely at my wrists. Blood flowed from deep cuts.

—*Don't wash yourself in the river. Don't let your blood drip into the river.*

With his hands cupped, he washed me at an appropriate distance from the river bank. While he was tending me, he talked: it was a pity that Nyembeti was retarded and scanty in her speech. For she had seen Juca Sabão being killed, she was the only living witness to the murder. But she wasn't credible. Which was why the murderers had spared her.

—*See what life is like. That girl's dim-wittedness isolated her from life. And now, that very condition has saved her.*

—*But has she always been like that?*

My father knew all about the girl from the cemetery. It was an old story: the girl had strayed from her life's path ever since she'd been born. Gossip had it that she took poisons. A day didn't go by without her swallowing a dose.

What was the reason for her vice? Well, some die in childbirth. Others die even before they're born. Like that little brother of mine who had never ascended into the light. With her, the same had happened. Her body had slipped out of the midwife's hands, and fallen into the sand. That was when a dark snake had appeared unexpectedly from the long grass. The type that didn't even need to bite you. It was enough to pass by within the width of a shadow and all living things round about lost their outer protection, grew thin and weak. The selfsame serpent did more than just pass by: it plunged its double fangs into

her, injecting her with liquids that then liquefy the victim.
But there was a surprise. For in her, it had the opposite
effect: the fatal bite had caused her to be reborn and to
blossom. It had been like a puff of breath, a kiss given to a
sleeping princess.

That was why it was said that her mother hadn't
delivered into light. She'd delivered her into shadow. Some
cry when they're born. They cry in order to learn how to
breathe. She breathed through others crying. When she
gave her her breast, her mother fell ill from the stickiness
produced by her lips. Her aunts came and their breasts
dried up until they looked like a pair of elbows. Unable to
take the succour of milk, she fed on poisons. They brought
it to her from the most diverse sources. That was the
reason for her vice. This also explained the difficulty she
had in expressing herself. The snake had tied a knot in her
soul, and had slithered into her voice.

—*Father, how is it possible that I dreamed about this?*
—*What do you mean, about this?*
—*I dreamed that Nyembeti had asked me for poison.*

My father shook his head and exclaimed: —*The things
that are entering your dreams, my son!* Men who live in a
continual state of shock leave their doors wide open when
they dream. It was through such a crack that ideas about
animals and the voices of the dead were infiltrating my
thoughts. Even that crazy girl, the witless Nyembeti, had
been allowed to establish herself in my soul.

But I know the reason for this dream.

For there was, indeed, a reason. I could no longer
remember, but as a little boy, I had played with the girl.

And I'd even hidden with her in half-concealed burrows.
My father had told me off, forbidding me to enter such
gloomy places. Those holes, he'd told me, are made for
creeping and crawling creatures, slimy insects, and animals
that have taken their leave of life.

All this, my father told me. Then he had ordered me to
return home. But before leaving, I shot him a comment as
if in payment for some term of affection:

—*Father Nunes likes you so much, Father.*

—*I know. I also know why he's leaving.*

—*He said he's tired. He's going to take a holiday.*

—*I don't even know whether he'll be back.*

As far as he could see, he was going away without any
destination in mind. After all, who does a priest confess
to? Does he speak directly to God? Our Nunes could never
confess to another priest, so alone was he. The problem,
according to my father, was that the cleric had some grave
sins to confess. Nunes had absolved criminals. The priest
had excused folk who carried more poison in them than
Nyembeti.

I returned to the house. At the entrance, Grandma
Dulcineusa seized me by the arm. Her affliction caused her
to blink hard, as if her eyelids were blinds being buffeted
by contrary gusts of wind.

—*Do you know what I suspect? I fear Miserinha may be
pregnant.*

—*How's that possible, Grandma?*

—*Haven't you noticed she no longer drinks water while
standing?*

—*Honestly, Grandma!*

—*Haven't you noticed she waits for her curry to get cold before putting it in her mouth?*

—*Grandma, do you know how old she is?*

—*She's been made pregnant by your grandfather, Mariano.*

—*Well now, that really is impossible.*

—*He's an old rogue, even dead, he still interferes with women.*

—*Miserinha's an old lady, Grandma, older than the earth.*

—*That grandfather of yours is such a charmer when he talks that he can make any woman feel younger.*

18 *The water aglow*

We look at a star as we look at fire,
Knowing that they are of the same substance,
but merely different in the distance
over which they consume themselves.
— *Aunt Admirança*

I was on the river bank, watching the women as they
bathed. They respected tradition: before entering the water,
each one asked the river for its permission:
   —*May I?*
   What silence answered them, authorising them to
plunge into the current? It wasn't just the local language of
which I was ignorant. It was these other idioms I lacked in
order to be able to understand Luar-do-Chão. To be able to
talk to my mother as she flowed by upon the waves, until
she became estuary.
   The women looked at me provocatively. Or
provocaptively, as my grandfather would say. They seemed
to have no shame. As far as they were concerned, their
breasts didn't warrant abashment.
   They weren't just amusing themselves. They were

fulfilling the ceremony that the medicine man had
prescribed in order that the earth should open again. The
curse that had befallen our Island could only be overcome
through a common effort. Everywhere one turned,
islanders were sending out signals of understanding with
the gods.

The women were wearing a string round their waists
that had been blessed. They were only allowed to bathe
on this side of the river. It was on the other side that the
tragedy had occurred, and that stretch of river had been
placed out of bounds for ever.

The unlucky incident was now a remote memory, erased
by the laughter of the women who dipped in and out of
the current like fish. I began to grow sluggish in the warm,
heavy air, when a sudden clamour made us jump. The
women rushed out of the water, some of them forgetting
to cover themselves with their capulanas. It was my Uncle
Abstinêncio who appeared, running in a panic. He paused
to gasp for air and then shouted:

—*Come on, something serious has happened! There's a
fire at the quay!*

We ran along the paths, in the lea of the hillside. Next
to the quay, there was a crowd, bustling excitedly. A boat
loaded with tree trunks was on fire by the quay. It was the
passenger vessel on which I had travelled. The whole thing
was ablaze, as if it was made entirely of flames.

—*Are there any casualties?*

—*Only Uncle Ultímio.*

—*Ultímio? Was he on the ship?*

—*He got burned as he tried to put out the fire.*

—Is it serious?

No one knew. He'd been taken home, and was being treated by Amílcar Mascarenha. My father signalled me to wait while he took a closer look at the incident. Maybe help was still needed.

I sat on the quay, watching the reflection of the flames in the water, like some silent play of light. Abstinêncio came over and sat down next to me. His sigh seemed almost to come from the ground:

—Serves them right!

He had no doubts: the fire was punishment, divine vengeance. They were cutting down trees everywhere, even the sacred forest had been chopped down. The Island had practically no shade. The administrator had a hand in the business, along with Uncle Ultímio and other powerful figures from the capital. They used the government-run ship for private cargoes of timber, and left the passengers stranded whenever they felt like it. Sometimes, even the sick couldn't be evacuated. In colonial times, Mariavilhosa hadn't been able to travel on the ship because of her race. Nowadays, passengers were excluded for other reasons.

—But, Uncle, isn't the shipping company state-run?
—And so what?

Abstinêncio had been warned about insisting that there should be a clear separation between private business and public obligations. He'd been dismissed when he demanded greater clarity in matters of payment.

I took advantage of my father not being there to seek some explanation regarding the accusations that I had heard but a short time before.

—*Uncle, tell me something: my father told me about an
incident with drugs and Juca Sabão's murder. He said that it
explained everything that was going on here.*

—*Your father is fantasizing. The folk who killed Juca were
arrested. They were put on trial and they're serving their
sentence.*

—*But isn't it true that a pistol disappeared from the
police station?*

—*That's true. But what does it prove? The guilty parties
confessed; they were people with a criminal record.*

—*Well then, why does my father stick to his version
of events?*

—*He always wanted to settle things by force of arms.
It came from his experience in the war. Your father thinks
everything can be resolved in that way.*

Fulano Malta thought that the world was so twisted that
a man couldn't be just in order to be good. Abstinêncio had
another explanation that didn't involve complicated plots:
what was happening now was something else.

—*See those flames mirrored in the river? Do you think it's
just a boat that's burning?*

Everything was being burnt by the greed of the new
rich. In his opinion, that's what was happening. The
Island was the opposite of a boat on a voyage. It was afloat
because it was heavy. Its folk were happy, there were trees,
it had animals and fertile land. When all this had been
taken away, then it would sink.

—*The Island is the ship and we are the river.*

We were interrupted by my father returning from the
quay, carrying a handful of ashes that he'd gathered from

the remains of the fire. He was going to sprinkle them over
the earth, I thought. But no. Fulano rubbed the palms of
his hands in my hair. I tried to resist. What was all this
about? Why was he anointing me with ash? My father told
me it was for my own good, to ward off bad spirits.

Afterwards, we still sat gazing at the quay. The fire had
died right down by now. How everything was consumed in
the batting of an eyelid, I thought. Fulano Malta seemed to
guess my thoughts:

—*Loss always happens quickly.*

—*I don't know whether I agree,* my uncle argued.

—*Take a son. Before we realise it, a son leaves home.*

We decided to go back to Nyumba-Kaya. Ultímio was
in a lot of pain. We gathered round his bed, accompanying
the doctor in his movements. Abstinêncio decided to break
the silence. He addressed my father:

—*Do you know something, Fulano? Standing around the
bed like this with Ultímio suffering, do you know what it
reminds me of?*

—*It's true, brother. I was getting the same feeling.*

Ultímio couldn't remember. He was still a child when he
suffered a serious accident and the whole family spent the
night awake, watching over him.

—*You were at death's door.*

Ultímio had fallen on some sharp nails while he was
fishing from a platform by the quay. He had almost bled to
death by the time he was found.

—*Do you know who saved you?*

Ultímio had no idea. Abstinêncio pronounced each
word like a hammer blow, slowly and deliberately:

—*It was a white man, brother.*

The man who saved him was a white, some stranger who was passing through the Island. It was he who gave him his blood, in sufficient quantity to fortify his whole body, as if he were to be born again.

—*Half the blood in your body is that of a white man.*

Ultímio dug his heels in, refusing to believe it. At first, he laughed. Then, he became serious and asked Abstinêncio to confirm it:

—*You're the eldest. Do you bear this story out?*

—*Yes, it's true, Ultímio.*

—*I don't believe it. You're telling me this now, when I'm lying here traumatised.*

And he went on complaining until Fulano, Abstinêncio and Amílcar left. We agreed that I would remain in my uncle's room to look after him until morning. I curled up in a chair, looking at the moonlight outside. The moon never gains such curves or appears so languid in the city. I was beginning to get dopey, almost succumbing to sleep, when Ultímio's words took me by surprise.

—*I wish you were my son, Mariano.*

I felt weak at the knees. I never expected such a statement from my uncle. I couldn't think of anything by way of a reply. It was Uncle who continued:

—*I'm not a happy person, dear nephew. My sons, I don't know where they picked up their ways.*

—*They don't often come here, do they?*

—*My sons can't come back to Luar-do-Chão. They'll never be able to come back.*

—*Why not?*

—*Do you remember Juca Sabão? Well, there are those who think my sons shot him.*

There was silence. All that could be heard was the ceiling fan.

—*And what do you think, Uncle?*

—*What do I think? I'm their father, Mariano. A father who wishes he had a son like you.*

Once again, the turning of the fan was the only, solitary noise. It was as if time itself were turning up there by the ceiling. As if the future were curling around, without an escape. After a while, Ultímio complained of pain. I gave him a glass of water and the medicine that had been prescribed for him. He calmed down, his groans getting ever fainter. Gradually, we both fell asleep.

In the morning, the doctor came to change the dressing. I sat there watching. While Amílcar Mascarenha busied himself with his treatment, Ultímio began to talk:

—*Last night, I couldn't sleep thinking of that story about the blood. Is it true, doctor, that I was given a white man's blood?*

—*I don't know what that is.*

—*You don't know what?*

—*A white man's blood.*

Ultímio settled himself more comfortably in bed, raising himself on his pillows. He refused the doctor's help, regained his energy, and once again addressed Mascarenha:

—*I like you. But my hatred of you is much older than I am.*

—*Are you talking about me or my race?*

—*I'm sorry, doctor, but for me, you are your race.*

—*Don't worry, Ultímio, I'm going back to the capital. You can rest assured.*

—*Are you going?*

—*Yes, I am.*

Ultímio started to fidget again in bed. Something had broken, deep inside his gaze. His voice seemed to have lost all its energy.

—*No, please don't go. I'm asking you, Mascarenha.*

—*It's no longer a doctor you people need.*

—*But stay, I beg you.*

Mascarenha pretended he hadn't heard, and put his equipment away in a box. Meanwhile, Ultímio altered his imploring tone, and took on an authoritarian air again:

—*In fact, you can't leave, Mascarenha, now that the ship has burned.*

—*There'll be another ship, that's for sure.*

19   A uniform returned

> When there was no ink left in the world, the
> poet used his own blood. Without any paper
> available, he wrote on his own body. And so,
> the voice was born, a river anchored within
> itself. Like blood: without a mouth or a source.
> — *A legend from Luar-do-Chão*

In Luar-do-Chão, people don't knock on each other's door
out of respect. Whoever knocks is already inside. That is,
he's already penetrated that private space, which is the yard,
the most intimate refuge of any home. That was why, upon
entering my father's yard, I clapped my hands and shouted:
  —*May I?*
  I was visiting Fulano Malta on the orders of Grandpa
Mariano. His instructions to me took up only a few lines:
—*Go to the store room and look for a black box which is on
a top shelf. Take the container to my son, Fulano.*
  There I was, then, lugging the box, waiting for my father
to summon me from the veranda. And sure enough, there
he was, cleaning his face with the sleeve of his shirt. He
screwed up his eyes, dazzled by the light, to see whether I

was alone. I entered the room, my feet picking their way through the general muddle. Before sitting down, I handed him the case.

—*It was Grandpa who asked me to give you this.*

He didn't seem surprised by the posthumous nature of the request. The contents seemed to intrigue him. He felt its weight, and then shook it to see what was inside.

—*I'm going to open it!*

His announcement of the act was a sign of his indecision. He was seeking my complicity. He opened it. Inside, there was a uniform, his old guerrilla's uniform. His reaction was a violent one, and he got to his feet, waving his arms:

—*I don't want this. I don't want this rubbish any more.*

—*All right, Father. Don't be like that.*

—*Where did he get hold of this?*

I shrugged my shoulders while he gave even more volume to his complaint. What was he going to do with this? Sell it to the Museum of the Revolution? Claim privileges, help himself to some land? What was he going to do? And who told me to go opening cupboards, the ones where we shut away the past? I should have surely learnt with him that you don't go around emptying your drawers. For he, Fulano Malta, knew only too well: there are cupboards that you open, but which give off thick steam and mists full of bad omens.

I didn't say anything, waiting for him to calm down. And that's what happened. Fulano sat down, looking vacantly at the uniform that was spread out on the floor. He looked at me as if I were a stranger.

—*Your grandfather didn't want to let me leave for the guerrilla war. Now he returns this to me?!*

It had been thirty years before that my father announced his intention to run away and join the liberation struggle. I wasn't even born yet. There was a meeting between the three of them: my father, my mother and Grandpa Mariano. My mother complained, in resignation. The reaction of the old boy was one of disbelief. Those who said they wanted to change the world merely wanted to take advantage of our ingenuousness to become our new bosses. Injustice was just changing hands.

—*It's not that I don't have faith in humanity. I just don't believe in mankind any more. Do you understand?*

And he spoke. Old Mariano spoke, using extensive arguments. That the world wouldn't change as a result of gunpowder. Other types of powder were required, of the sort that explode so benignly within us that the only sign of their presence is a scarcely noticeable shudder in our way of thinking.

—*If you want to change the world, you've got a whole world to change right here in Luar-do-Chão.*

—*I'm going, Father.*

And the reason for his decision was summarised right there in a simple pamphlet that he took out of his bag, all dog-eared. He went over to the light of the oil lamp and read it slowly and deliberately:

—*'It's not enough that our cause should be pure and just. Purity and justice must exist within us.'*

—*It was a good man who wrote that. But he's alone.*

And Fulano continued, elaborating on his reasons. That

all those who were unhappy had joined together and were moving the world towards another future.

—*I fear that future, my son. A future made by the unhappy?*

Grandpa had got to his feet, confident in his convictions. He knew mankind from observation. And these people were no different from those he'd known before. We start off by believing they're heroes. Afterwards, we accept them as patriots. Later, that they're businessmen. And finally, that they're no more than thieves.

—*Not everyone is like that, Father.*

—*For me, it's enough that just one of them should be pure.*

That was their conversation of thirty years before. My father remembered it as if he were still arguing the case with his old father. He recalled it all out loud. But he wasn't talking to me. He was addressing the uniform lying sprawled across the floor. I tried to alleviate his sadness, offer a shoulder for him to lean on.

—*That's Grandpa for you, you know only too well.*

—*That's true. In the end, no one can lose their temper with that man, Mariano.*

—*Do you believe that he died when the photo was taken, Father?*

—*So has he died, then?*

—*Well, that he ended up like this, then...*

He wasn't sure. Maybe his end had begun before, on the eve of the fatal photograph. Among Mariano's mannerisms was the one whereby he never used a wardrobe to hang his only dark suit in. He hung it from a hook in the ceiling,

just as you do with clothes when you live in a hut, out
in the country. None of us could believe it: with built-in
cupboards and countless hangers, what was the sense in
keeping his clothes suspended from the ceiling?

—*Like this, I don't have to fold it, and I avoid creases.*

—*Oh! Come on, Father!…*

—*And apart from anything else, the suit catches
the breeze.*

No clothes should remain motionless, growing old in
the dark. Exposed to the light, the gentle breeze gave the
outfit a life of its own. When this happened, Grandpa was
absorbed by the sight of his clothes moving and swinging
uncannily. Then, he would say:

—*There go my clothes, out for a stroll.*

When old Mariano had asked for help, that afternoon,
in unhitching his suit from the nail, a cold shiver ran
through the family. He put it on in front of everyone. And
he never took it off again.

—*So, aren't you going to unbutton yourself, Father?*

—*Tomorrow, we're going to take a photo, with all the
family together. Like this, we'll save time.*

And he went to bed fully dressed. Everyone in the house
was scared. As if we were aware that he was saying his
farewells, by putting on his final suit of clothes. For he had
veered towards the slovenly of late. Sometimes, he'd even
gone out into the street in his pyjamas. Grandma would get
very agitated. But he replied:

—*If death is a long sleep, then I'm dressed for it.*

My father smiled, captivated by the memory. We could
have sat there for ever, recalling stories about the old man.

But it was getting late, and Fulano Malta accompanied me to the door. He was carrying his guerrilla's beret, with its red star stitched on to it.

—*Do you want it?*

Before I could answer, he tossed it to me. I placed it on my head jokingly. My father couldn't even raise a smile. He looked at me, but didn't see me. He was absent, carried on a wing of sadness. He who had fought so hard to create a new world, had ended up without a world at all.

—*To be honest, I'm sad because I was never a father.*

—*Didn't you have me?*

—*Ah! Yes, of course. Don't take any notice...*

20 *The revelation*

Everyone discovers their angel by
having an affair with the devil.
— *Grandpa Mariano*

—*Where did you find that beret?*

Ever since visiting my father, I'd forgotten about the
beret stuffed on my head. Grandma Dulcineusa peered at
the adornment suspiciously. Did she recognise it?

—*I found it in the lumber room.*

What lumber room? That place I called a lumber room
had been empty for a long time, exposed to the mice.

—*What do you mean there's no longer a room? You gave
me the keys, Grandma, and they were the only ones that
fitted a lock.*

—*Then you say I'm the one who's mad?! That room
doesn't even have a door, or floor, or anything at all.*

As I was insistent, she led me to the place. Dulcineusa
was indeed right. There was no door, and the floorboards
had been ripped up. There were some loose planks, like
bones stripped of any flesh, and that was all that was left.
My eyes flashed along the hall to try and make sure. This

was certainly the room where I had made passionate love, where I had conjured up clothes and even memories of clothes.

—*But Grandma, I'm sure...*

—*Come, dear. Come with me and I'll make you some tea.*

She tapped me on the forehead, as if consoling me for some fit of craziness. Then she let out a spontaneous, fruity roar of laughter. It was a long time since I'd seen Dulcineusa so happy. She sang to herself and danced her way down the hall. Only one name blossomed on her lips: Mariano, Mariano, Mariano. She claimed that she had met him, and thanked me for delaying her quasi-late husband's funeral.

—*You just can't imagine it, my little Mariano! It's been better than before, when we were alive.*

—*You're alive, Grandma. Don't forget that.*

—*I'm with him, lock, stock and barrel. Only now am I sure that he's mine, and mine alone.*

—*What about Miserinha? I haven't seen her for some time.*

—*Miserinha's gone; she went back to her own house.*

Our visitor had taken her leave some days before. The tubby lady had walked into the room and announced her intention of leaving Nyumba-Kaya.

She'd dragged herself off to the room where Mariano's body lay, with Dulcineusa's permission, and kissed Grandpa on his forehead, saying:

—*Thank you, Mariano. I'm grateful. But I feel better in my own dark corner!*

Then, she'd torn a piece of the sheet on which Grandpa

rested. She took that torn piece of cloth off with her, in order to stitch together her memories in her own home.

Miserinha's departure had ultimately been a comfort for Dulcineusa. For she was now alone, without having to compete with her old rival. Grandma had rediscovered Mariano's own exclusive love for her.

After drinking my tea, I went out to the lagoon at Tzivondzene. It was there that the liquid remains of my mother and little brother were buried. At the edge of the water, there was no sign marking the place where they were buried. I sat down there, in the heavy silence of the afternoon. And I recalled my mother, Dona Mariavilhosa. Now I knew her story, it was like a dagger thrust to my conscience. How could I have been so unaware of her suffering? Mariavilhosa's life had become a hell after she had given birth to the dead child. She had become a condemned woman, the bearer of bad luck, watched carefully by the others so that she shouldn't spread her ill fortune through the town. The unborn child was a *ximuku*, a drowned creature. That's what they call the stillborn. My little brother had been born without saying a word; he'd brought with him a secret that he'd taken away again.

My mother had remained in a state of impurity. My father had opposed strict observance of tradition. But there was still some resistance within him to turning the page on time-honoured precepts. Mariavilhosa was forbidden to touch food. She avoided entering the kitchen. If she so much as picked up a plate, she had to cleanse her hands. It was said that she should 'burn' her hands. She would warm her arms over an open fire so that the stain of her tragedy

would not contaminate the food. And as she was excluded
from the kitchen, I never remembered her bustling around
with the other women by the stove. Even in her speech,
she followed traditional directives. Mariavilhosa spoke in a
low tone, so low that she could barely hear herself. She no
longer helped out in the fields. Her impurity might affect
the whole land and inhibit the plantations from bearing
their crops. My mother had ended up like an old cargo
ship. She was carrying too much sadness to remain afloat.

A hamerkop flew over my head. It landed and came
towards me, without showing any fear. It stood there
contemplating me serenely, as if I were familiar. I felt like
touching it, but I sat there without moving. It snuggled
into itself, as if it were going to sleep. I closed my eyes, my
strength sapped by the peace and quiet. When I got to my
feet and tip-toed over to try and rouse the bird, it remained
motionless. I wondered whether it might not be sick. Does a
bird fall sick? Or does it plunge straight into death, without
going through the intermediary of an illness? Encouraged
by the bird's attitude, I eventually touched it, brushing it
lightly with my fingers. At that point, dozens of other similar
birds were liberated from the heron's body, in an explosion
of wings, beaks and plumage. And in a thick flock, the birds
flew off, skimming across the waters of the River Madzimi,
there where my mother had been turned into water.

Night had fallen when I returned home. I looked
for Dulcineusa, for I wanted to tell her about what had
happened with the bird of portent. She wasn't in her room
or in the kitchen. I surprised her in the parlour, lying in
the dark next to Grandpa. She had her back to me, and was

half undressed. Her blouse was unbuttoned and her back
was gleaming, dotted with beads of sweat. They seemed to
have just made love. Grandma was still breathless. I was
afraid she'd remain there, exposed to the cold and mist. I
called her affectionately:

—*Grandma Dulcineusa!*

She turned round slowly. I almost fell to the ground
with the shock of it. It wasn't Dulcineusa. It was my aunt,
Admirança! And her breathlessness wasn't the result
of fatigue, but she was weeping. Hand in hand, fingers
intertwined, blind to the world. She was weeping next
to Mariano.

—*You just don't know how much I loved this man!...*
How much I still love him.

—*Grandpa?*

—*This man isn't your grandfather, Mariano.*

She got up and left in tears. I stood there in the dark,
devoid of ideas, deserted by all feeling. Mariano wasn't
my grandfather? Had I heard this correctly? Or was my
aunt already contaminated by the death that hung over the
house? The shadow of the hamerkop crossed the surface
of my soul.

I returned to my room and sat down at the table. I
gazed at the blank sheet lying in front of me. There was
nothing written on it. Had there ever really been words
written there? I picked up the pen. My hands were ablaze
with desire, but at the same time, fear paralysed me. It
was a deep apprehension that something was reaching its
climax. I began to write, my hand obeying an ancient voice
as I composed:

*Forgive your Aunt. But there is still something I
have to reveal to you: Admirança was the woman in
my life. It wasn't Dulcineusa, or Miserinha, or any
other. It was she, Admirança. She is much younger
than her sister, Dulcineusa. When I got married, she
was far from womanhood still. She was a little girl,
the youngest of Dulcineusa's sisters. Later, she became
shapely, her flesh curvaceous. You can't imagine
how beautiful she was! She lived together with us
under the same roof, and Dulcineusa never suspected
how much her sister filled my heart and flavoured
my dreams.*

*Dimira, that's what I used to call her. My
Dimira, my dearly beloved! As a young girl, she was
in the habit of jumping in a dugout and paddling
up the river. On moonless nights, Admirança would
push the boat out until she'd almost lost her footing.
Then she would jump into the boat and, as she
moved away from the shore, she would start to take
her clothes off. One by one, she would throw each
garment into the water, and pushed by the current,
they would reach the shore. That's how I knew
when she was completely naked. But this happened
when I could no longer see the boat, lost as it was
in the distance. As I couldn't see it, I imagined her
nakedness, and promised myself that one day, that
woman would be mine. And it was as if, at that
very moment, a flash of light opened up the darkness.
I was able to ignite the night.*

Not a new moon went by when I wasn't peering

*from the river bank at her invisible presence. On
one occasion, I received a warning: a crocodile had
been seen following the boat. The beast, so they told
me, must belong to someone. I could imagine who
that might be: Miserinha. That woman had powers.
Out of jealousy, she had decided that her rival,
Admirança, must die, out there in the placid waters
of the Madzimi. In a panic, I ran to Miserinha.
And I ordered her to suspend her spell. She denied
everything. To tell you the truth, she didn't even hear
me. She was possessed, guiding the monster through
the darkness. I couldn't contain myself: I hit her
on the back of the neck with a pestle. She collapsed
immediately, like some torn sack. When she awoke,
she looked in my direction as if she couldn't see me.
The blow had taken away her power of vision. From
then on, all Miserinha could see were shadows.
Never again would she be able to lead her crocodile
through the waters of the river.*

*I thought Miserinha would begin to hate me. The
following day, she left our house. She pulled me into
a corner and asked:*

—Are you frightened I'll take revenge on you?

—I know you have the powers to do so...

*—Don't worry, Mariano. A man who can love
like that can only inspire respect in his other women!*

*That night, I went back to the river and found
Admirança still in the dinghy. She thought I had
come seeking her body and kisses. But no sooner
had I boarded the craft than I threw myself on my*

*knees before her, begging her to let me sleep there
with her. To sleep, without more ado. That I had
never slept with any woman before. She looked at
me, incredulous, as if the absence of moonlight had
clouded my judgement. She held out her hand to me,
helping me to lie down in the bottom of the boat.
And cradled by the waves, I fell asleep.*

*In the meantime, Admirança was sent to Lualua,
where there was a Catholic mission. We would meet
each other there, not a month went by without our
doing so. That was how she became pregnant. But
she couldn't have a baby. I quickly thought of a way
of cleansing the sin. I asked Mariavilhosa, your
mother, to pretend that she was pregnant. If she
played her part well enough, the spirits would later
give her a child of her own. And so your mother
put on such a convincing show, that her belly began
to swell.*

*Your mother was growing from nothing. Your
father was all smiles with satisfaction. And even
she believed that she was harbouring some new
offspring. Meanwhile, in the mission at Lualua,
Admirança gave birth to a child. We brought the
little baby back under cover of night and pretended
that a birth was taking place in Nyumba-Kaya.
Even your father wept, convinced that the newly
born was fruit of his own flesh and blood.*

*But as time went on, the little boy grew and
began to take on features of his own. Admirança
grew thin worrying that the boy might reveal his*

*father's true identity. She begged me to allow this son
of hers to leave the Island. Let him grow up outside,
far from sight. And far from her guilty conscience.
So the boy was sent to the city. There, he became a
man, a man sure of his feelings. That man is you,
Mariano. Admirança is your mother.*

*This was the lie that closed up the earth, causing
the ground to refuse to receive me. But it wasn't
just this deception. There's another matter, another
shameful aspect to my life. I scarcely have the courage
to confess it. But I know I have to do so, and to
write it all down in your handwriting. That's the
only way that I shall purge the shadows of my
existence.*

*So let me continue in chronological order. As you
know, Fulano Malta, the man who believes he is
your father, came back from the guerrilla campaign,
bringing with him two pistols. He kept them as
a souvenir of the times. It had a meaning for the
dreams he had had. One night, I discovered the
place where these arms had been hidden, underneath
some old floorboards. I went there and pinched one
of the pistols. I didn't know what I was going to do
with it. But I was sure it would bring me in some
money for some urgent things I needed. So I had a
word with my grandsons, Ultímio's sons. At that
time, they still lived in the city, for it was before they
went abroad. People said they had veered towards
evil deeds, that they stole cars and burgled houses
over there in the city. I called them to Luar-do-*

*Chão and sold them the gun and its ammunition.
They paid me for it promptly, and everything was
agreed without any more being said. A blood secret,
a family matter.*

*Do you know what I suspect? That it was that
same gun that killed my friend Juca Sabão. He
was almost certainly eliminated with the help of
my greed. For it happened that, next to my friend
Sabão's body, they found the gun, the same gun that
belonged to my son, Fulano. They took the pistol to
the police station. That same night, I couldn't get
to sleep, consumed by the thought of it all. Could I
allow suspicion to fall on my own grandchildren?
Or on Fulano, the owner of the gun? Was I going to
betray my family in order that justice should be done
on behalf of my friend?*

*This is what I did: I broke into the police station
and took the gun without being seen. I threw it into
the river that same night. Bu something happened
that I could never have predicted: instead of sinking,
the pistol stayed afloat, spinning madly as if caught
in some infernal whirlpool. And suddenly, as if an
invisible finger were pressing the trigger, shots were
fired up into the clouds. Flashes of lightning still lit
up the sky when I took to my heels and ran back to
Nyumba-Kaya.*

*During all this time, I remained in a sort of
blessed ignorance over who had committed the
murder. I preferred it this way: to believe what the
courts said, and go along with appearances. But this*

illusion never left me in peace with myself. Neither me nor my ancestors dwelling in the ground of time. The earth can never swallow the thorn of such a lie. Now, I bear witness to this unhappiness on the sheet of paper, as if I were tearing up the silence in which I preserved the unfortunate memory.

Let me ask you this, Mariano, my son: did I kill Juca too? Perhaps. Or maybe we all helped in this crime, by agreeing to remain silent. What I should have done was to overcome my fear, go out into the world and tell all that I had been witness to. Given myself up for having hidden the evidence. But no. I was governed by my lesser instincts. You know something: a cowardly man sweats even in the water. I bowed before my false conscience. Remember my shame and tower above my own weakness. As if you were climbing steps carved into my back.

Having got this off my chest, for the first time I can sign off honestly and in full:

Your father, Dito Mariano

PS. Now take me down to the river, for my time has come. Ask Curozero to help you. I don't want anyone else there. Neither relative nor friend. No one. Do you remember where your mother's waters and the body of your little still-born brother were buried? Next to the lagoon that never dries up. Well, I want to be buried next to the river. Ask the gravedigger, Curozero. He'll tell you. That's where I should be buried. I'm someone who died badly. Have you seen

any rain these last few days? Well, I'm the one who
stopped it raining. It's my fault that the moon, the
mother of rain, has lost its potency.

Do you know something, my little Mariano?
When you were born, I called you 'Water'. Even
before you were given a person's name, that was
the first word I used on you: madzi. And now,
I'm calling you 'Water' again. Yes, you are the
water that follows me, wave upon wave along the
current of life.

My moment has passed. You are here, the house
is at peace, the family prepared. I've already taken
leave of myself, so that I don't need me any longer.
You'll see now that the waters will be released from up
there, on top of the clouds. You'll also see how the earth
will open once again, offered up like a womb from
which everything is born. I'm now completely dead,
unburdened by lies, without the guilt of falseness.

Do me a favour: place the letters I wrote in my
tomb, lay them on top of my body. Let's pretend I'm
going to read them in my new abode. I'm going to
read them to you, not to myself. After all, everything
that I have written has been done second-hand.
Your hand, your writing, have given me a voice.
You alone composed these manuscripts. I wasn't the
only one responsible for dictating them. It was the
voice of the earth, the river's turn of phrase. What
I remembered came through from before I was
born. Like that dead star we still see because its
light reaches us late. Within me, even that gleam

*has faded away. Now, I have been authorised to
become night.*

*After this, go and call Curozero Muando. And
take me to the river. Let's take advantage of the early
hours of the morning, always a good time to be born.*

Outside, the night was losing its thickness. I jumped
over the wall of the house, looked back, and unable to
contain my surprise, what did I see? The roof over the
reception room now back in place. The house was no
longer defending itself from mourning. Nyumba-Kaya was
cured of death.

A hint of blue on the horizon revealed that morning was
rising. I met Curozero Muando coming out of his house.
He was walking towards me, his spade over his shoulder.

—*I knew it! I knew you were coming to call me! Let's go
quickly. No one must see us.*

Shielded by the dark's secret, we brought the dead man
down to the river. I was astonished at how light Grandpa
Mariano was. We took him to the river wrapped in his old
sheet. There, on a bend of the Madzimi, Curozero stopped,
almost repenting.

—*It's here.*

—*Shall we bury him where the water's flowing?*

No. Grandpa was going to be buried on the bank, where
the soil was abundant and soft. Curozero shovelled up
spadefuls of sand so easily that his actions seemed unreal.
It began to rain the moment we laid Grandpa in the earth.
I had the letters in my hands, but the sheets of paper began
to fall even before I managed to throw them into the grave.

—*Curozero, help me to pick these papers up.*

—*What papers?*

Only I was able to see the papers fluttering about, falling into the ground. How could the gravedigger be so blind to such visible occurrences? I picked up the letters one by one. And it was then that I noticed something: the writing was fading, becoming liquid, and the paper soaked, dissolving into nothing. In an instant, I was fingering no more than absence.

—*What papers?* Curozero insisted.

I responded with a silent, empty-handed gesture. The gravedigger sprinkled the sides of the hole with water, and we covered the grave with earth. Muando, barefooted, stamped on the ground, smoothing over the sand. Then, he spread some ubuku grasses, the sort that grow along the river-bank, on top of the grave. Finally, he gave me a reed and told me to stick it at the head of the tomb. It was from a reed that Man was born. We were re-enacting the origin of the world. I stuck the wild reed into the ground good and deep. Like a flag, the reed seemed proud, pointing up at the sky.

—*Now, let's wash ourselves in the river.*

We dived into the waters. I don't know how we washed ourselves. For me, the river was so dirty that it could only make us dirty too. But I carried out the ritual, exactly as required. We cleaned ourselves with the same piece of cloth. Then, Curozero held up a burning blade of elephant grass, shaking it and pointing it at the four compass points.

—*Your grandfather's opening up the winds. The rain's nice and loose. The earth's going to conceive.*

21 *A key made of rain*

This is what I learned over in those
valleys where the sun sinks: after all,
everything is light, and if people are lit up,
they do so through others. Life is a fire;
we are just its brief incandescences.
— *João Celestioso's words upon returning*
  from the other side of the mountain

It hasn't stopped raining ever since the funeral. In the
fields, there's so much water that puddles have proliferated
in their thousands. White dust undulates on the surface
of the water. It's as if the earth were vomiting the white
powder that Juca Sabão had carelessly chosen to sow.
Who says the earth always swallows up without spitting
anything out?

I travelled the Island under the rain. My clothes,
soaked through, were so heavy that it was as if they were
wearing me. I was impelled by a strange force, as if destiny
were taking me by the hand. I knew exactly where I was
heading: I was going to see Miserinha. I looked through
her window, and there she was, pretending to sew, seated

in a big armchair. I recognised the cloth: it was the piece
of shroud that she'd torn off on her last visit to her beloved
Mariano. From this tiny piece, she wanted to rebuild the
whole thing. Until she too could lie on top of the sheet and
float away on infinite waves.

The fat lady seemed aware of my presence. She asked
'who's there?' and I, in order not to make her anxious,
presented myself. She smiled and summoned me into her
dark little room.

—*You're very light of step*, she commented. —*You walk
like an angel.*

And she bent to pick something up from under her
chair. It was the colourful handkerchief she had with her
on the ferry crossing to Luar-do-Chão.

—*This handkerchief fell into the river. How come you
have it here, Miserinha?*

—*Everything that drops in the river is brought to me.*

—*Don't tell me it's the crocodile that brings things to you.*

—*What crocodile?* asked Miserinha, letting out a laugh.
And she immediately added: —*You're beginning to pay too
much attention to the stories you hear on the Island...*

I looked at the sheet in her hands. The thread was a
web of confusing cross-stitches. When it came to it, not so
different from her life. She waved the handkerchief that she
had offered me as protection against the spirits:

—*You don't need this bit of cloth any longer, young
Mariano.*

We talked about this and that, merely so that time
would take notice of us. When I got up to leave, Miserinha
thanked me for having reconciled her with the family

abode and for having allowed her to take her leave of
Mariano. When referring to Grandpa, she would say 'my
Mariano'. And she went on repeating 'my Mariano' while
she stitched the cloth, as if it were a scar on her memory.
I crossed the doorway quietly, leaving the old woman
absorbed in her shadows.

I passed by Fulano Malta's veranda. I would always call
this man 'father'. The house was empty. Where could the
old guerrilla fighter have gone? I walked up to the birdcage.
I could still imagine the little bird inside it: the door open,
but the creature there, of it own volition and at its own risk.
In fulfilment of the immutable and sacrosanct. The cage
turned from prison into a home, the bird residing within,
without having lost its ability to fly.

I was alerted by some noises in the yard. My former
father appeared from the back of the house wearing his old
guerrilla uniform. We laughed.

—*Are you in training, Father?*

—*This uniform doesn't fit me any more. Look…*

He held his stomach in to see if its roundness could be
adjusted to his own rotundity.

—*What are you celebrating?*

—*Celebrating? Only if it's life itself.*

He sat down on the step, unbuttoning the tunic so that
he could feel more comfortable.

—*Do you remember that time I visited you in the city?*

He knew that he must have embarrassed me. But I
had to understand: he had never lived. The city was the
territory of others whom he envied to the full. And who
made him suspect that time was a ship that always left

without him. On the shore where he remained, all people could do was to say farewell.

—*You didn't embarrass me, Father. I even hoped you'd return.*

And we laughed. I could see he wanted to hug me, but as he was about to, he held back. I told him I had to go, and dusted off my trousers with both hands.

—*Wait. Don't go without taking this!*

Fulano Malta got up and went to fetch a cloth bag. He dragged it along the ground, revealing its considerable weight.

—*What's this, Father?*

—*Open it and you'll see.*

I pulled the string and opened the bag. Inside were books, my long-lost study books. He'd been keeping them for years. For years, he'd borne the guilt of a lie that he himself had created: my study manuals never had been thrown into the Madzimi.

—*Now, Father, I'm the one who's going to throw them into the river.*

He saw the joke. But his laughter faded away and his lips curved away in sadness. He knew why I was there. It was to say my goodbyes. At last, he hugged me.

—*Just as you were teaching me...*

—*Teaching you what?*

—*To be a father.*

As we separated, his tunic fell to the ground. I bent down to pick it up. But he stopped me. I should leave it where it was, for it was the last time he'd wear the uniform.

I looked back again. Fulano was waiting there, certainly

waiting for me to turn. For he was waving his arms to attract my attention. He took the cage and threw it up into the air. Before my astonished gaze, the cage changed its shape and turned into a bird. When its transformation was complete, it flew off into the sky and vanished from sight. I was no longer pained by that nightmare in which the house rose on the wing only to fade away, a cloud among other clouds.

I went back to Nyumba-Kaya. The kitchen was full of light and sitting next to the stove were Grandma Dulcineusa and Aunt Admirança. They were looking through a family album.

—*Come, Mariano, come and have a look.*

This time, the album was full of photographs. There was old Mariano, and there was Dulcineusa too, receiving gifts. And amid it all, among so many pictures, there was a photo of me in Admirança's arms.

—*Look at us, Mariano.*

She raised her arm to give me her hand. I wanted to speak but found myself unable to call her 'mother'. I hugged her as if it was only now that I had come home. Grandma interrupted us.

—*Stop this. No one would believe you were an aunt and a nephew. Mariano, look what your Grandpa Mariano left me.*

And she held out her hand. On one of her fingers she wore a ring that glittered, star-like. The ring was such a dominant presence that for a moment her fingers seemed to have recomposed themselves, slender and with their original shape. Dulcineusa sensed that I was about to leave and ordered me:

—*Don't forget to water the house when you leave.*

The house had regained its roots. It therefore made sense to relieve it of its dryness. Admirança got to her feet, took my hands in hers and spoke in a whisper, as if she were in some sacred place.

—*We've already spoken to Fulano. he's going to move in here, into Nyumba-Kaya. We'll be protected. Don't worry. And the house will be protected too.*

She inspected my fingernails. They were still full of soil, the dark sands of the river. Even so, Admirança kissed my hands. I tried to pull my arms away, saving her from getting dirty.

—*Don't worry, Mariano. This soil is blessed.*

—*Mother?*

—*No, your mother died. Never forget it.*

I took my leave by kissing her on the brow. I left with a feeling of emptiness, as if I had no set route to follow. But I still had further visits to make. I made for my eldest uncle's house. The road opened before me as if I were obeying some internal torrent and the landscape were taking on surreal contours. I was walking towards Abstinêncio's abode. Through the window, I could see what looked like a party. I could hear music. Had Uncle returned to life's pleasures? I looked in and smiled. It wasn't, after all, one of his usual orgies. There was just one couple dancing round the room. Abstinêncio was dancing, his partner in his firm grip. Who was his companion? I stood on tip-toe to try and glimpse who my uncle's dancing partner was. And that's when I realised: there was no one else but himself. Abstinêncio was dancing with a dress. That same dress: the dress that belonged to Dona Conceição Lopes.

I crept away slowly so as not to deprive him of his dream. But Abstinêncio saw me through the window and came to the door. He called me.

—*I'm happy, dear boy. Dona Conceição is here with me, she's moved to Luar-do-Chão.*

—*So I see, so I see!*

—*Conceição is so proud of me.*

—*Really, Uncle?*

—*It's that I couldn't keep it to myself, I told her everything.*

—*Told her what?*

—*That I was the one who set fire to Ultímio's ship. It was me.*

His finger on his lips was a request for secrecy. Abstinêncio further confided: he had spoken to his brother, Fulano Malta, and they would all go and live at Nyumba-Kaya. Now, he could leave and visit the world. He was at peace with himself, his fears of old laid to rest. A childish laugh was his excuse to go back inside. Someone was waiting for him inside, and he resorted to a half-hearted gesture by way of goodbye.

And so it was through that world, which seemed to have grown, that I continued my journey. Never before had the Island seemed so extensive, so much so that it seemed larger than the river itself. I descended the slope until I saw Ultímio seated on the harbour wall. He was gazing at the other bank of the river. The bandages that covered his burns seemed to give him an inner sadness. It was as if he were expecting me, for he began to talk with his back still turned:

—*I'm waiting for the boat. I'm going to the city.*

—*Are you leaving, Uncle?*

—*Yes. But I'll be coming back very soon to buy up Nyumba-Kaya.*

—*Do you not realise, Uncle, that you can't buy the old house?*

—*Now listen here, I'm going to buy it with my own money. That house is going to be mine.*

—*That house will never be yours, Uncle Ultímio.*

—*No? And would you mind telling me why not?*

—*Because that house is me. You're going to have to buy me to gain possession of the house. And for that, Uncle Ultímio, no amount of money will be enough.*

My reaction astonished him. And justifiably. If I hardly recognised myself, standing up defiantly to an older relative, Ultímio clicked his tongue on the roof of his mouth to show how irritated he was.

—*You think we're the generation that betrayed everything. Well, you're going to see the generation that follows. I know what I'm talking about...*

—*This generation you're talking about, I'm also part of it.*

As I walked away, he remained seated, looking disconsolately at the waters of the river. I was some distance away, when he called me:

—*Mariano!*

—*Yes, Uncle.*

—*Your grandfather was right to choose you! You're a true Malilane.*

A tractor was approaching. To my utter surprise, it was being driven by the gravedigger, Curozero Muando. When he saw me, he had some difficulty in braking the vehicle and more still in turning the engine off. The machine ran up onto the verge and came to a halt when it ran into some bushes. From the height of his improvised throne, the gravedigger addressed me:

—*See? I'm now working for your Uncle Ultímio!*

My wealthy uncle had given him a job, along with a thousand promises. He was to take charge of chopping down the trees, and in return he would gain numerous privileges. I didn't know what to think of this man Curozero Muando, who had seemed so worthy, with such a sad memory of his father's murder, and who now agreed to be ordered around by Ultímio. Curozero defended himself:

—*You know, Mariano: a goat has to eat where it's tied up.*

—*You're a person, not a goat.*

—*Who knows? Maybe I'll chop down that jujube where your grandfather was put to sleep. It must be worth a bit, mustn't it?*

He laughed. He was only joking, he said. What was this? Had I lost my sense of humour? he asked. He turned the steering wheel this way and that, like a child at play. Then he looked at me, all serious. I hadn't understood all that he could do. In the intervals between loading up timber, how many private deals of his own could he make? All in secret and informally. Privatisation begins at home, a bit here, a bit there. Some are eaten up by poverty, others are swallowed up by wealth.

Wearily, I interrupted him:

—*And what about your sister, Nyembeti?*

She was going to take his place in the cemetery. Over the years, his sister had learnt the secrets of the profession. She had been prepared for it in mind and body.

—*Go to the cemetery. As a matter of fact, she asked after you.*

—*Did she?*

—*What I mean is that you know she says things without really saying anything at all.*

He started up the tractor again. And off it went, ganda-ganda-ganda, in the noisy rhythm that earned it its name in the language of Luar-do-Chão. The noise of the ganda-ganda faded into the distance, while I made my way to the cemetery. Previously, it made me anxious that there were no signs of a city, no street corners, no streets in a straight line. Now, wherever I looked, all I wanted to see was bush. No lawns or flowerbeds, or well-kept gardens. All I wanted were bushes sprouting up spontaneously, wild undergrowth, trees that no one had planted, ground that no one could pollute or pillage.

I arrived at the cemetery. A bush was rustling noisily. I jumped with fright. A hamerkop was taking off. It flew over me, curious. I looked at its beak to see if it was carrying anything. Legend has it that the bird takes bones from graves, and that it flies off loaded with cloth, fingernails, and teeth. And it would even take a tibia for a perch. But this particular bird was clean and it flew away singing. Until the sky swallowed up the winged creature

The cemetery was deserted. I shouted Nyembeti's name. Then I heard her muffled voice. I looked around but saw no one. Her voice seemed to come from the depths of the earth. Had the beautiful girl turned into a root? Or worse, into a lost soul? I walked along among the graves until I found her: Nyembeti was deep inside an unfinished grave. She was digging away about two metres down.

—*So the earth's no longer closed, Nyembeti?*

She nodded, and to emphasise the point, she crumbled some soil between her fingers. That was the most important piece of news. The ground had opened up, the sky had unfastened itself. The bird of portent had been right.

The gravedigger asked me to come to the edge of the great hole. As I approached, I was attacked by giddiness and I was vaguely aware of stumbling into the abyss. Far from the light of day, I felt the gravedigger pulling me to the bottom of the tomb and there, under the gently falling sand, she threw herself upon me. I was lying on my back, while Nyembeti's silhouette showed against the descending light. The sky was no more than a tiny rectangle. It was like being in the roofless room back at home. So that was it: this was my final dwelling place and the hole above was the missing roof through which the house breathed. And I couldn't see anything else. I was blind, darkness took me over, shadows penetrated my ears and all my senses. I could still feel Nyembeti's nakedness adjusting to my body. The last thing I could confirm was that there's nothing hotter than a mouth. No fire can match the fever of two bodies in the act of love.

I woke up, unaware of how long I had been absent. Nyembeti was sitting there and was passing a damp cloth

over my face. I smiled. A vague memory of a small boy's
laugh drew itself mistily upon my mind: I was playing
at the bottom of a grave with another child. In my
recollection, I didn't get as far as putting a face to it, and I
was too tired to elaborate on this particular ghost.

I spread the cloth out and Nyembeti squeezed it over
her chest. I watched the water dropping, like a string of
beads, upon her breast. And I wondered to myself: was I
condemned to love this woman only during the dizziness
of a dream? But then I understood: I could never possess
that woman as long as I didn't take possession of that land.
Nyembeti was Luar-do-Chão.

22 The last letter

I'm like the word: my greatness is
where I have never touched.
— *Grandpa Mariano*

I lay under the great jujube tree on the banks of the
Madzimi. The river is gentle here, curved like a rounded
elbow, almost as if in self-reproach. This was the tree where
Grandpa Mariano would come and idle away the time. I
call him 'Grandpa' but now know that he is my father. But
for me, Dito Mariano will always be my grandfather. And
so that's how I recalled him, ancient and eternal, as he
lay down under the branches of the jujube. With his back
resting against time, old Mariano would help soak up the
sunset. As he used to say: the evening is a sleepy creature,
and it needs somewhere damp and soft to lie down. The
burial of the sun, like that of a living creature who hasn't
managed to die completely, needs damp soil, sand that has
been fertilised by the river that causes all to be born.

Resting there in the shade, it wasn't the absence of
the most senior of the Marianos that pained me. What I
missed was our secret correspondence. Those letters had

spawned a more intimate grandfather, of a sort that I could more readily call my own. By writing through my fingers, he began to be a father to me, while I was reborn into another life.

The letters induced in me a sense that I was transgressing my human condition. Mariano's manuscripts fulfilled my most intense dream. After all, the greatest aspiration that man can have is not to fly. It is to visit the world of the dead while surviving to return to the territory of the living. I had become a traveller between these worlds, setting off along hidden roads and through mysterious mists. It wasn't just João Celestioso who had gone beyond the last mountain. I had been there too.

I no longer cared about trying to explain how Mariano had written those lines. I just wanted to prolong the daydream. As I lay under the jujube, I could hear the breeze blowing through the branches that provided my shade. A large leaf fell onto my chest. I touched it as if I were stroking Grandpa's hands. Gradually the green drained away and the leaf grew pale, its colour faded. I picked it up from the ground. It wasn't a leaf but a sheet of paper. And its threads were lines and letters. My trembling hands were holding Dito Mariano's last letter:

My dear Grandson,

Now you know where you can visit me, I no longer need to write to you by means of calligraphy. We can talk here, in this shade where I can gain dimension, a body reborn into another body. You, my dear Grandson, fulfilled your cycle of visits. You

*visited house, earth, man, river: the same being, the
only difference being in the name. There is a river
born within us, it flows through our house and flows
not into the sea, but into the earth. That river some
people call life.*

*This is my last visitation. After this, there will be
no more letters. We'll have plenty of opportunities to
visit each other along these paths. What's for sure is
this: in this shade which, after all, lies within you
alone, you can reach the other bank, beyond the river,
at the rear end of time.*

*Everyone needs great causes; people need a
country to be proud of; they need God. But not me.
This tree was enough for me. It's not one of those
domesticated trees you find in gardens. Just like me,
this tree hasn't been taught its culture. What it has
learnt, it has absorbed from its rustic sap. What it
knows comes from the River Madzimi. Far from
the river, the jujube dies. That's what makes it
divine. That's why I never failed to come and pray
in its shade. So as to learn from its eternity, to gain
a long-distance heart. And to get ready to be born
again, through seed and rain.*

*Come and lie down here. You'll see that sleep here
on the edge comes as a result of the most profound
indolence. I'm now asleep well beyond slumber itself.
Sleeping is a river, a river made only of curves and
calm waters. God is on the river bank, watching
from his window. And envying our journeying,
infinitely, through life and beyond. Hence God's*

*fatigue. That God of Father Nunes is consumed
by suspicion. He's been obsessed with controlling
his work for centuries, along with his regiment
of angels. Our God doesn't need to be present. He
left after he had completed his job, confident in its
perfection.*

*I've told you everything about the family, I've
unravelled stories, undone the knot of untruth. Now,
I'm no longer going to risk being ambushed by a
secret. The hunter sets fire to the grass through which
he moves. I do the same with the past. Time that
has passed, I kill as I go along. I don't want to leave
anything behind me, for I know there are creatures
that settled there, in times gone by.*

*At long last I'm free of that slumber that tied
me to the sheet on the big table. You can't imagine
how much I wearied of that room, how tired I was
of the visitors who kept arriving, feigning sadness.
Where were they when I was alive and kicking, and
in need of support? Why were they now assembled
together in a show of tears and prayers? Didn't you
think it too much fuss for such limited ends? Well,
let me give you the answer: it was fear. That's why
they came. It wasn't death that they were scared of,
but the dead man I am now. They feared the powers
I gained by crossing that last frontier. Fear that I
would throw their lives into disarray. That's what I
made you aware of, dear Grandson. If I call you 'my
dear Grandson', it's a weakness of expression. You
are my son. My grandest son, for you were born of a*

boundless love. For that reason, I didn't choose you to preside over the ceremonies of my passage to the other shore. You chose yourself alone, life wrote my own name inside your name.

In these manuscripts, I have managed to purge myself. Those who attended my wake were suffering from delusion: that man lying on the sheet looked like me. But it wasn't me. The dead man was someone else, at the end of another life. I am just using death in order to live. You, my son, you were right: death is the scar on a wound that was never inflicted, the memory of an existence we led from which all traces have been erased.

During those days, when I lay in the room without a roof, I was contemplated by moons and by stars. Sometimes an unremitting chill would descend into me. I had visions of the deepest depths: the abyss that no bird ever crossed. And me falling, forever falling. From rock to stone, from stone to grit, from grit to the deepest cavity of nothingness. But then, I sensed you arriving, my son, and my head began to tap your fingers: and you began to write my letters. I was sustained by a simple conviction: no one was ever going to bury me. And that's what happened. It was I who walked into the earth under my own steam. And I laid myself to rest just as the evening does in the watery bed of the river. More ancient than time itself. More distant than the furthest horizon. There where no home ever fertilized the soil.